Day Leclaire invites you to a wedding...

The Location: the Cinderella Ball.

The Bride: Ella Montague. She had grown up with fairy tales, but this year was her last chance to meet her handsome prince and live happily ever after.

The Groom: Rafe Beaumont. He didn't believe in fairies, hope or marriage. He had come to stop the Cinderella Ball once and for all, until he discovered an even better way to exact his revenge—a SHOTGUN MARRIAGE to Ella Montague!

And it could be your own!

On one very special night, single people from all over America come together in the hope of finding that special ingredient for a happy ever after—their soul-mate. The Cinderella Ball offers the opportunity for immediate matrimony: come single, leave wed. Which is exactly what is about to happen to three unsuspecting couples in Day Leclaire's magical new trilogy:

FAIRYTALE WEDDINGS

Titles in this series are:

Dear Reader,

Ella Montague grew up on fairy tales and happily-ever-after endings. So is it any wonder that she would expect the magic of the Cinderella Ball to work for her? Unfortunately, Rafe Beaumont doesn't believe in faith or hope or miracles. Worse, he's determined to prove how wrong Ella's dreams are by making this the very last event of its kind.

I've really enjoyed writing the Fairytale Weddings series. And I hope you'll enjoy sharing in the romance and fantasy of the Cinderella Ball just one more time.... A very happy, healthy and prosperous New Year!

Day Leclaire

P.S. My next book, *The Secret Baby*, will be out in May!

Books by Day Leclaire

HARLEQUIN ROMANCE

3028—JINXED
3139—WHERE THERE'S A WILL
3183—IN THE MARKET
3238—A WHOLESALE ARRANGEMENT
3285—TO CATCH A GHOST
3301—ONCE A COWBOY
3338—WHO'S HOLDING THE BABY?
3361—MAIL-ORDER BRIDEGROOM
3376—ONE-NIGHT WIFE
3404—MAKE-BELIEVE ENGAGEMENT
3433—TEMPORARY HUSBAND
3438—ACCIDENTAL WIFE

Day Leclaire
Shotgun Marriage

Harlequin Books

TORONTO • NEW YORK • LONDON
AMSTERDAM • PARIS • SYDNEY • HAMBURG
STOCKHOLM • ATHENS • TOKYO • MILAN
MADRID • WARSAW • BUDAPEST • AUCKLAND

To Kathy Smith Acosta. Thank you so much for always
being there when I've needed you.

And to Susan Ashmore Fairbank, who exemplifies faith,
hope and incredible courage every day of her life.

ISBN 0-373-03440-7

SHOTGUN MARRIAGE

First North American Publication 1997.

Copyright © 1997 by Day Totton Smith.

PROLOGUE

The Montagues—Forever, Nevada

"YOU'RE dreading tonight, aren't you?"

Ella Montague glanced at her mother, reluctant to hurt her feelings with an honest reply. To be precise, she'd been dreading this evening's Cinderella Ball for five long years—ever since the last ball her parents had thrown. For on that bleak night, all her hopes and dreams had been thoroughly shattered. But to admit that aloud and risk causing her mother pain... She shook her head. She just couldn't do it.

"I know how much this occasion means to you and Dad...." she offered cautiously.

"The Cinderella Ball does mean a lot to us," Henrietta conceded. "It's our dearest wish that others experience the sort of love and joy your father and I found in our marriage. That's why every five years we sponsor these balls—why we've kept the tradition going for thirty-five years." She reached for her daughter's hand. "But you must know that what we want most of all is for you to be happy."

Happy? Ella's fingers trembled within her mother's grasp. What had once seemed such a certainty crept ever closer to the realm of impossibility. "Maybe some of us weren't meant to find 'happily-ever-after,'" she whispered.

"Of course you were." Alarm filtered through her mother's voice. "How could you think otherwise?"

5

Ella bowed her head. "I'd always imagined I'd meet the man of my dreams on a night like this, that we'd fall in love and marry in the space of one magical evening. Just like you and Dad. But maybe—" She fought for control, fought to voice a possibility her parents had always refused to face. "Maybe the Cinderella Ball doesn't work for everyone."

"It works for those who believe," Henrietta insisted.

"Does it? Are you certain?"

Sadness crept into Henrietta's gentle blue gaze. "That Beaumont man hurt you badly, didn't he?"

"I'll survive," Ella said with a shrug.

"Not a day goes by that your father and I don't regret that night. It's all our fault. We should have known..." Her hand fluttered in the air like a wind-blown butterfly. "We should have realized..."

"You weren't to blame," Ella instantly denied. "No one could have known what Rafe's sister intended to do. Shayne never told any of us what she'd planned. Besides, I didn't fall in love with Rafe at the Cinderella Ball."

"You just lost him there," came the shrewd observation.

There wasn't any point in denying it. "I'm not a naive twenty-one-year-old. Nor am I a starry-eyed dreamer." Ella lifted her chin and met her mother's gaze resolutely. "Not anymore." The past five years had seen to that.

Henrietta's breath caught in dismay. "You've stopped believing, haven't you? Oh, darling, you mustn't give up."

"I haven't." Thick, dark lashes fanned Ella's cheeks. Not yet.

Not unless tonight ended those few remaining dreams of finding an everlasting love. She'd give it a final chance, a last Cinderella Ball in which to find her Prince Charming. And if it didn't happen, she'd know. She'd know that she wasn't one of the special people meant to find that pot of gold at the end of the rainbow, one of those who discovered the "happily-ever-after" that turned fantasy into reality.

She stood, despair tarnishing the amber clarity of her eyes. Over the past several years she'd made up her mind. If daylight broke and she remained unwed, she'd face the inescapable truth. She'd accept that heaven never met earth. That stars were but distant pinpricks of cold firelight rather than vehicles for wishes. And that fairy godmothers didn't help dreams come true, even for little girls named Cinderella. She'd finally concede that Rafe had been right all along. Fairy tales were just pretty stories and most people never lived happily ever after— her parents the one exception that proved the rule.

"Ella? Please tell me the truth. You do still believe, don't you?"

She turned and offered her mother a reassuring smile. "It's all right. I still believe." For this one last night, she'd cling to the wispy remains of her hopes and dreams. She'd give the magic of the ball a final opportunity to work.

"I have to be certain you haven't given up," Henrietta said anxiously. "It's so important to me ... to us."

"I know." Ella's smile grew. "You and Dad are incurable romantics. You always have been."

"There's no point in denying it," her mother confessed. "But that's not why I'm so concerned. There's something else. Something I haven't told you."

Ella's amusement turned to alarm. "Mother, what is it?"

"Sit with me, darling. We need to talk."

The Grand Hotel—Forever, Nevada

"You're looking forward to tonight, aren't you?" Rafe cradled the phone receiver against his ear with an uplifted shoulder. "You wish me to lie about it, Shayne?" he demanded, stabbing a heavy gold cufflink into the buttonhole of his stark-white dress shirt. "Shall I wrap up the truth in pretty falsehoods so you'll feel better about what I intend to do?"

"Yes! That's exactly what I want."

"You know I don't operate that way," he retorted flatly. "Now, did you phone from Costa Rica just to give me a hard time? Or is there something important you wish to discuss? I have a party to attend."

"Darn it all, Rafe! This *is* important. Please. Promise me you'll leave the Montagues alone."

"You know I can't make such a promise."

Distress crept into his sister's voice. "You mean you won't."

"Fine. I won't." He gave the words a finality she couldn't mistake. "The Montagues are going down and I intend to be there when it happens. Hell, I plan to be the one to push them off the cliff."

"But it's my fault! How many times do I have to tell you that?"

He stared down at the thick gold-embossed envelope he'd tossed to the bed. It contained his sister's "ticket" to the ball. "Maybe I would have found a different approach if it hadn't been for this latest incident. That affair five years ago was bad enough. But for them to have the unmitigated gall to send you another invitation..." He heard the trace of Spanish accent seep into his words and his hand tightened around the receiver as he fought for control, fought to chain the black fury that rode him so relentlessly. Only the strongest emotions caused him to regress into childhood habits. "That I cannot forgive."

"Don't you understand? I wanted to attend tonight's ball. I thought... Maybe..."

Rafe gritted his teeth. "You'd hoped *he'd* be there."

She didn't reply, but the heartbreaking catch in her breath bled through the static on the line.

"Ah, *pobrecita hermanita*," he whispered. "Your pain is mine. I would do anything to spare you more hurt." He shut his eyes, a fierce determination taking hold. "And so I shall. I will resolve this matter once and for all. When I have finished with the Montagues there won't be any more Cinderella Balls to tempt you or anyone else with romantic rubbish."

"Please, Rafe." Emotion choked her words, adding to the burden of guilt he'd carried for five impossibly long years. "Don't do it."

"I must," he replied with devastating simplicity. "They cannot continue to play games with innocent lives. They cannot steal people's money with promises of love and happiness and then deliver nothing but pain and misery."

"You have to believe me. It's my fault, not theirs. How can I convince you?"

"You can't, Shayne, for one simple reason." He gazed out the window of his suite, watching as the sun surrendered its light and warmth to the greedy demands of the desert. "The fault is mine more than anyone's."

"I...I don't understand."

"You spent half your life with no one to care for you. When I finally found you, I swore I'd protect you." His mouth twisted. "It was a promise I failed to keep. I can't change the past. But I can make sure it's never repeated. I won't fail you this time."

She tried to muffle her sobs, but he heard them, the sound of her grief, soul-crippling in its impact. "We need to talk," she finally managed to say. "You don't understand."

"Ah, but I do, *mi pichón*," he replied calmly. "I understand more than you'll ever know."

Gently, he cradled the receiver. His gaze returned to the envelope on the bed and he picked it up. Inside he found a white velvet pouch that held a surprisingly heavy "gilt" ticket. He pulled the metallic wafer from its nest. It caught the last rays of the setting sun and shimmered as though alive, flooding the suite with a bright, golden promise.

"I swear to you, Shayne," he murmured. "They will pay."

CHAPTER ONE

The Montagues' Cinderella Ball—Forever, Nevada

LIKE a hungry mountain lion scenting its prey, awareness of Ella struck first, alerting Rafe to her presence long before he zeroed in on her location. His movements slowed as he approached and tension rippled along the length of his shoulders, radiating downward into his arms and fisted hands. He caught tantalizing glimpses of her through the line of people waiting to enter the Montagues' ballroom—the brilliant flash of her gold dress, the deep luster of ebony hair, an endless expanse of magnolia pale skin.

And then the crowd shifted and he saw her.

His reaction came hot and swift, with all the raw power of a jaguar coiled to spring. Desire and a driving need to possess clawed through him, making a mockery of the indifference he'd thought he'd attained over the past five years. The rational part of his brain might reject her, Rafe realized bitterly, but the baser, more instinctual part still wanted her with a ferocity he couldn't deny.

Memories long suppressed flooded his mind and fed his fury—a fury aimed squarely at himself. *Dios!* To his disgust he couldn't drag his gaze from her. Five years ago he'd thought her the loveliest woman he'd ever seen. Since then she'd matured into a beauty beyond even his fertile imagination.

He shifted to one side of the line, allowing the glittering tide of guests to pass him by as he battled to overcome the perversities of fate and human nature. He was suffering from a nasty case of lust, no more than that. It had to be lust, he refused to consider any other possibility. It was a natural reaction, one any red-blooded man would feel toward such a woman. He'd worry if he didn't have a need to hold Ella in his arms, to seduce her into his bed, to join with her in the most ancient of rituals. Still, he'd be a fool if he didn't acknowledge that this overpowering urge would complicate his mission. His craving for her could go no further—not after what she'd done...and not considering the fate he had in store for her.

Even as he made the determination, an alternate plan occurred to him, one that would satisfy his thirst for vengeance as well as his hunger for possession. He watched Ella with cold silver eyes as he analyzed this latest possibility. Assuming she hadn't changed since the time he'd known her, it just might work.

A humorless smile crept across Rafe's mouth. For the sake of his sanity, it had better work.

Ella had lost track of how much time had slipped away since the start of the Cinderella Ball. But she'd felt the loss of each precious moment. More than anything she longed to steal from her place in the receiving line and fight for her last chance at happiness. Instead, she greeted the guests with a warm smile and collected the gold metallic wafers that served as tickets to the ball. They went into the velvet-lined basket she held, building into a miniature gold mountain of fervent dreams and wishes. And as each ticket landed with a melodic clink she added her own silent prayer that this guest would find his or her heart's desire.

She glanced up as the next visitor approached and summoned another smile. He was a large, good-looking man whose tired hazel eyes warred with a determined expression. "I'm Jonah Alexander," he introduced himself. "Listen, I have a small problem—"

But even as he began his explanation, an odd frisson of awareness caused her to glance past him. Past him . . . and straight into the diamond-hard gaze of Rafe Beaumont.

"Hello, Ella," he said, the softly spoken words at direct odds with the threat glittering in his stormy gray eyes.

The blood drained from her face. It couldn't be Rafe! Not here. Not now. Not on the most important night of her entire life. The basket tilted in her unsteady grasp and tumbled to the floor. For an instant, she couldn't react, couldn't move, could only stare at Rafe in disbelief. She dreaded to consider what secrets she gave away with that one single look. Knowing his uncanny ability to read her every thought and feeling, it had to be far too many. She didn't regain control until the man at the head of the line went down on one knee and began scooping tickets back into the basket. With a muffled exclamation she crouched beside him.

"Are you all right?" he asked in an undertone.

What had he said his name was? Joe Something? Jonah? That was it. Jonah Alexander. "I'm fine," she insisted, though she suspected her trembling hands betrayed her. Gathering up the last ticket, she stood. "Thanks for your help."

"My pleasure."

Jonah rose, too, and glanced pointedly behind him. If he'd thought to intimidate Rafe, he soon learned his mistake. Rafe folded his arms across his chest and held his position as though he had all of eternity to wait. But it was the expression in his cold, bleak gaze that worried Ella the most. She'd seen that look before, had seen men of immense wealth and power cave before it, wilting like unwatered daisies beneath the fierce desert sun. Without uttering a single word he made it clear that Jonah was intruding on a personal matter.

To her amazement, Jonah shrugged off the look. Using his height and breadth to secure his place at the front of the line, he turned his back on Rafe. "Anything else I can do for you?" he offered.

Despair filled Ella's eyes. "I'm afraid not. Welcome to the Cinderella Ball. Enjoy your visit and we wish you a..." Her voice wavered, but she recovered swiftly. "We wish you a joyous future."

"You're certain?"

Rafe stirred behind him. "Tell him to go, Ella. You know this is a private matter."

She gave her self-appointed protector a reassuring smile. "Rafe and I are old..." She hesitated, her smile turning bittersweet. "We're old associates. But thanks for your concern."

Jonah inclined his head, conceding defeat. Sparing Rafe a final look of warning, he exited the reception line and plunged into the crowded ballroom.

"A friend of yours?" Rafe asked, stepping forward to take Jonah's place.

"I've never seen him before in my life." She lifted a shoulder with an air of hard-won indifference. "I guess he just recognizes trouble when he sees it."

For the first time, a hint of amusement lit Rafe's silvered eyes. "And I am trouble?"

She stilled, searching the taut, uncompromising lines of his face. "I don't know. Are you?"

"I can think of only one way to find out."

Ella nerved herself to ask, "Which is?"

Cold resolve supplanted his earlier amusement and she shivered at the change. "Be my escort this evening. Then you will have the answer to your question."

His tone made it a demand, not a request. Nor did she miss the underlying threat—*refuse at your own peril*.

The line of guests waiting to enter the ballroom had begun to build. She needed to end this unexpected confrontation and soon. "What do you want, Rafe?" she questioned in a low voice. "Why are you here?"

"I'm a guest, of course." His gaze held everything but innocence. "Why else would I attend?" Then he opened his hand to reveal a ticket. The thin strip of gold gathered in the overhead lights, reflecting each one with blinding intensity.

"You're here to find a wife?" Ella whispered, stricken.

"Isn't that the purpose of tonight's gathering?" With a flick of his thumb, he sent the metallic wafer spinning skyward. The ticket arced through the air, a thousand bits of fire splintering along its length. It landed square in the middle of her basket with a resonate clink.

"Welcome to the Cinderella Ball," she murmured automatically, unable to tear her gaze from his ticket. *Rafe had come to find a wife!* How could she bear it? How could she stand aside and watch as he chose from the vast array of beautiful women attending tonight's ball? She lifted her gaze, anguish clouding the amber clarity of her eyes. "Rafe—"

He closed the polite gap between them, trespassing on the protective circle of air most people hesitated to violate. But then, Rafe rarely concerned himself with what "most people" might do. Nor was it the first time he'd violated her space—just the first time she didn't welcome the encroachment.

"Join me," he murmured. "Assign this duty to another and dance with me, *amada*."

"I can't." She fought to keep her voice steady and impersonal. "I have an obligation."

"You are lying, Ella. It isn't obligation that keeps you here, but fear." The words were spoken so only she heard, the breadth of his shoulders concealing her dis-

tress from the prying eyes of waiting guests. "You will
have to face me sometime. Why not get it over with?"

"What do you want?" she repeated. "If you've come
to find yourself a wife, why bother dancing with me?"

"This is not an issue I care to discuss in front of others.
When will you be free from your duties?"

Never! "It may be some time," she began, before
reconsidering.

Tonight represented her last chance for true happiness. She was still determined to give herself every opportunity to meet the man of her dreams. But how could
she do that with Rafe in the vicinity? How could she
stand aside and watch as he selected a wife? Worst of
all, how could she possibly find love when the man before
her still held that love tight within his grasp. Until she
resolved the situation with him, she'd never be free. And
until she was free, she couldn't risk her heart again.

"Come, *amada*," he insisted. "Come with me."

As though in a trance, she inclined her head. Turning
to an attendant stationed nearby, she surrendered her
basket. "Could you take over, please? I need to help this
guest." And without a single murmur of protest, she
allowed Rafe to take her arm and lead her away.

He didn't speak again until they were on the dance
floor. Catching her surreptitious glances, he lifted a sooty
eyebrow in question. "Have I changed that much in the
past five years? I suspect I have, considering the way
you keep looking at me."

"I suppose so," she conceded, using the excuse to
study him more thoroughly. "Somewhat."

With his jet-black hair and piercing gray eyes, she'd
always considered Rafe dangerously attractive while not
quite understanding why. But tonight she saw him with
the eyes of a woman, recognizing what she'd been too
young to comprehend before.

How innocent she'd been not to see the unbridled passion that fired his spirit, she marveled, or the raw sensuality that was as much a part of him as bone, muscle and sinew. And yet, perhaps she'd been fooled by the remote wariness with which he shielded his innermost emotions, the cool control he used in his dealings with those who came within his sphere of influence. She found it a deadly combination. He lured his victims with the white-hot blaze of passion while his arctic stare warned that he'd not be easy to tame.

"Well?" he prompted. "Are the changes so bad?"

She tilted her head to one side, daring to tease, "You have a few more wrinkles." Of course the lines bracketing his mouth and creasing the corners of his eyes only emphasized his natural strength and maturity. "And you're going gray at the temples."

"Age has a way of doing that to a man," he replied calmly.

A faint laugh escaped her. "It has a way of doing that to all of us." Her laughter died, replaced by a sadness she couldn't conceal. "I suppose the most obvious change is that you've gotten harder, if that's possible. Colder."

His arms tightened. "Don't blame age for that."

"No," she whispered. "I'm to blame, aren't I?"

He didn't deny it, but cradled her in his arms as though she were precious to him instead of a woman he despised. It was too much. She couldn't bear to be this close to him and know he didn't share her feelings. She had to end this moment.

"You said you wanted to talk," she reminded.

"First we dance." His widespread hand filled the hollow at the base of her spine, stirring emotions that should have died long ago. "Then we'll talk."

Ella closed her eyes to block out the sight of him. But it only intensified her awareness. Without sight, other senses came to the fore. She could hear him—the subtle give and take of his breath close to her ear, the exultant singing of her silk dress against his tux. His unique scent wrapped itself around her, a blend that made her think of wind and rain and rich, fragrant earth. And the feel of him... The muscles beneath her hand rippled as he moved, reminding her that he wasn't a man of leisure, but one who worked the land, who came by his physique through years of backbreaking labor rather than from a high-tech gym. Finally, the only sense left unsatisfied was taste. And just the thought of closing her mouth over his, of rediscovering the distinctive flavor of him was almost beyond bearing.

Her eyes flew open and she focused on the crisp bow tie at his throat. She forced herself to concentrate on that and only that, to ignore the other sensations rioting through her. Not that it helped. To her horror, the temptation to tug at the ends of his tie, to rip open his shirt and taste the strong, tanned column of his throat nearly consumed her. Five years ago, she'd wanted him with all her heart and soul. And now... She trembled in his arms.

Dear heaven, she wanted him still.

"What is it, Ella?" he murmured. "What are you thinking?"

How could she answer when the truth was the very last thing she should entrust in his care? Fear urged her to run, just as desire compelled her to stay. Fear won the battle. With an inarticulate murmur, she pulled free of his arms and darted around the other dancing couples, desperate to escape. She didn't understand her reaction to Rafe any more than she understood his reason for attending the ball. Both defied explanation.

The garden seemed the safest retreat and she took the back staircase from the ballroom. Already guests were making their way to the library where the county clerk busily processed marriage applications. Ella mustered a smile of greeting as she passed, envying the happiness radiating from the fortunate couples soon to be wed.

Bypassing the dining area and buffet tables, she continued through the French doors opening onto the garden. A pathway led off to the left, the trees and shrubbery glittering with fairy lights. She turned in the opposite direction, slipping between an almost indiscernible opening in the bushes. Safe from prying eyes, she wrapped her arms about her waist and bowed her head, allowing the pain to consume her.

Rafe followed Ella at a discreet distance. It wasn't difficult to keep track of her. Her gold gown provided a shimmering beacon to hone in on. He lost sight of her when she entered the garden, but by then he knew where she'd gone. If he hadn't been through the gap between the shrubs before though, he'd never have found her. Even armed with that knowledge, he wasted several precious minutes uncovering the narrow opening.

This place would serve him well tonight, he decided. Besides offering privacy, it would allow him time to determine a course of action without the threat of outside interference. He and Ella had often hidden from prying eyes within the shelter of the Montagues' "privacy glade," a small grassy area, surrounded by thick bushes.

He'd come to Nevada for a short visit—to attract investors for a hotel he'd hoped to build on the west coast of Costa Rica. And he'd hired Ella as his temporary assistant because she'd gotten along so well with his sister, Shayne.

It was the worse decision he'd ever made.

Ella had been a starry-eyed, twenty-year-old embarking on her first job. The attraction between them had been instant and mutual. The three months he'd in-

itially planned for the trip had stretched to six months
and then to a year.

Those had been special times, times when he'd taken
her in his arms and kissed her until the world melted
from existence. Back then, their love had seemed more
constant than the dry desert winds and far fiercer than
the scorching midday sun. How he'd wanted her! His
need had become a desperation, a narcotic that had
briefly seduced him into believing that magic and miracles could exist.

What a fool he'd been.

Taking a deep breath, he forced the memories from
his mind. To dwell on such things now would only
weaken his resolve. And he'd waited far too long for this
moment to allow that to happen.

He stepped from the concealment of the bushes into
the glade and that's when he saw Ella. A sledgehammer
to the gut couldn't have had a more crippling impact.
For what seemed an eternity he fought to keep his knees
locked in place, fought to force the air in and out of his
lungs, fought to rein in emotions he'd believed forever
denied to him. But his control slipped from his grasp
like starshine through open fingers.

Maldito! Never had he seen such a sight. If the heavens
above had parted long enough for one of their denizens
to slip to earth, she could be no more pure of feature
or blessed with grace than this woman before him. For
the sake of his eternal soul, he should leave her untouched; he knew it as well as he knew his purpose for
being here. But he was a man, not a saint, with a man's
need to seize and possess. So he remained, absorbing
the perfection of what soon would be his.

Moonlight washed her ebony hair with silver and gave
her skin a pearly iridescence. Her Grecian-style gown
clung to the supple lines of her body, lines that had both
ripened and grown more defined over the past few years.

The softness of youth had been transformed into the lean fluidness of womanhood. Her breasts were fuller, her narrow waist flaring into shapely hips and a firmly curved backside.

His hands closed into fists as he fought to gain mastery over the heat pooling in his loins. He wanted her, wanted to reacquaint himself with every inch of her. Only one thing kept him in place. She stood with head bowed as though in defeat. He'd thought he could come here this evening, that without a shred of emotion he could destroy the woman who'd caused his sister so much pain.

But seeing Ella, defenseless and vulnerable, in pain herself, he found he couldn't. He couldn't take the path he'd originally planned. Not yet. Not until he'd determined whether she felt a shred of remorse for her actions five years ago. Perhaps if such an emotion eluded her, he'd be able to carry through with his intentions.

He must have made some small sound for she stilled. With all the elegance and caution of a woodland deer, her head lifted and she turned to face him. For an endless moment their gazes met and held—the hungry, ruthless eyes of a predator locking with the wary topaz of the prey.

She held something in her hand, a shimmering strip of gold that she swiftly pocketed in the pleated folds of her gown. He couldn't be certain, but it looked like one of the tickets to the ball. "You shouldn't have followed me, Rafe," she stated in a low voice.

"I had no choice." He approached, skirting the ring of moonlight that encircled her. "You felt it, too. Didn't you, *mi alma*?"

"Don't call me that." Golden sparks leapt to life within her fiery gaze. "I'm not your soul. How could I be, when you have no soul?"

His mouth twisted. "I don't doubt you're right. But that doesn't change a rather bitter truth."

"Which is?"

"You still want me."

The breath shuddered from her lungs, the fragmented sound disturbingly audible in the stillness of the night. "I wish I could deny it," she retorted, before falling silent. Then she squared her shoulders, her mask of composure slipping back into place. He was impressed. She accomplished a feat few could have managed considering the stress of the moment. "I wish I could deny my feelings," she repeated. "But I can't."

The dense shadows concealed his satisfaction. "No more than I can deny wanting you." He'd surprised her, his frankness slipping beneath her defenses to touch the vulnerability he'd witnessed earlier. He lifted an eyebrow. "You don't believe me?"

"It seems ... unlikely."

"Why? Because we're at odds over this Cinderella Ball?"

"Yes."

His laughter held little humor. "Do you think desire is like a light switch? Do you think it's an emotion that can be turned off with a flick of the finger? Is it like that for you?"

"No."

The bleakness in that one single word impacted with devastating force. He didn't want to acknowledge her distress. But how could he avoid it? She stood so alone, a fragile captive held within a prison of moonlight. And all he had to offer was a different sort of prison—one where they shared their captivity. Unable to refrain, he reached into the silvery pool of light and caught her hand, drawing her toward the momentary freedom of the shadows.

"Desire, *mi alma*, is like an uncontrollable hunger. It must be fed before it can be sated."

He brushed his thumb along the tender fullness of her lips. They parted and for a hot instant he thought she meant to take him into her mouth. Then she turned her head as though denying her need. Deliberately he cupped the curve of her cheek, forcing her to look at him.

"We never fed that hunger," he told her. "We never feasted on our passion. Never satisfied our appetites. And now we're starving, dying for a taste of forbidden fruit."

She didn't relent. "Then we'll have to starve. Unlike Eve, I refuse to be tempted."

"You want me to seek satisfaction elsewhere?"

She flinched as though she found his words painful. "Then you were serious? You're here to find a wife?"

"I'm thirty-five years old. Don't you think it's time?"

"I'm the last person you should ask. Although I'm curious." She slipped from his grasp, distancing herself from him physically, if not emotionally. "Why come here to choose a wife? Considering how opposed you are to the Cinderella Ball, I'd think this would be the last place you'd pick."

He gave her the truth. "I came to resolve the situation between us. I can't move forward until I've put the past where it belongs. In the past."

Tension radiated from her. "What do you mean? How do you intend to settle our differences?"

"For a start, I wish to spend the evening with you. We could...talk."

"No," she instantly protested. "Not tonight."

His eyes narrowed at the hint of desperation he sensed behind her words. Closer scrutiny was in order here. "I'm afraid I must insist," he said with a negligent shrug. "You would be wise not to refuse me."

"And if I do?"

"Then I will choose my own method of resolving our...differences. One less to your liking, I fear."

Still she stood her ground, fixing him with an unflinching gaze. His admiration for her strength and perseverance grew. She'd always been a determined woman, one who didn't back away from adversity. More often than not, she chose to champion the underdog, a circumstance that had caused conflict in their relationship. Oddly, it pleased him to discover that she'd held to her convictions.

"Why come forward now, Rafe?" she demanded. "Why after all these years?"

"Is my timing bad?" he asked in mock innocence.

"It couldn't—" Her breath caught for a revealing instant. "It couldn't be worse."

He frowned, hearing again that note of desperation. Something was very wrong here—something more than just his presence—and he was determined to discover what that might be. "Is my timing bad because it interferes with the Cinderella Ball?"

"Isn't that reason enough?"

"Possibly..." His suspicion grew and with it his certainty that she was concealing something from him. "Or is there another reason, one you prefer to keep from me?"

Her pulse fluttered at the base of her throat, capturing his attention. "There's nothing," she whispered, a hint of despair flitting across her delicate features. "Not any more."

Then it came to him in a white-hot flash. "*Madre de Dios*! There is more."

"No—"

"Don't lie to me! You were planning to marry this evening." He caught her shoulders in a bone-crushing grip. "Weren't you?"

For a moment, he didn't think she'd answer. Then her chin tilted and she looked him square in the eye. "Why so shocked? Wasn't that your plan, as well? You've suggested as much.''

He forced himself to ease his hold, to caress the bared shoulder beneath his palm instead of crushing it. Something felt off kilter, but he couldn't seem to work through his fury to discover what. ''Why, Ella?'' he questioned gently. ''Why would you do such a reckless thing?''

''Reckless? The Montagues' daughter meeting the man of her dreams at the Cinderella Ball isn't reckless.'' An impenetrable calm encased her as she spoke, an icy reserve he felt compelled to breach. ''I find it quite appropriate.''

''Don't be ridiculous.'' Anger flashed within his silver gaze. ''There's nothing at all appropriate about marrying a man you've only just met this evening. And you damned well know it. If I had my way there would be no more Cinderella Balls.''

''I'm well aware of that. I'm also well aware that you've done everything within your power to bring an end to them.''

A humorless smile cut across the angled planes of his face. ''Not everything, or I wouldn't be here.''

''What do you mean?''

He sensed her alarm, but did nothing to ease it. ''I mean there were one or two methods I chose not to implement.''

''You mean you choose not to implement them...*yet*.'' He inclined his head in agreement and her mouth compressed. ''I'm surprised you were willing to show such restraint.''

''I prefer to employ less absolute options,'' he retorted. ''Unfortunately, they haven't worked. Which leaves me with a small dilemma.''

Ella lifted a dark eyebrow. ''Is that so? You amaze me. In the past you never would have hesitated to do your worst. Don't tell me you've learned compassion or forgiveness in the past five years."

He tugged her closer, bitterly amused when even that failed to intimidate her. But then, why should she fear him? No matter how angry he became, he could never harm her. She had to know that. "If I'm a man without compassion or forgiveness, you have only yourself to blame."

A surprising softness glistened within the tawny depths of her eyes. "I don't believe that anymore than I believe you'd carry through with the various threats you've made over the past few years."

"That may prove a costly mistake on your part." He allowed a grim warning to infuse his voice. "The fact that I have not exercised all the options at my command shouldn't be mistaken for weakness, *mi amada*."

She laughed at that, the sweetness of the sound quenching a lengthy drought. Once upon a time he'd lived to hear her laughter. But he'd purged that need long ago. His mouth compressed. Too bad abstinence hadn't purged his other needs as well—the ones that demanded a more physical expression.

"Trust me, I've never considered you weak. Far from it." Her amusement faded, replaced by an apprehension he was hard-pressed to resist. "Why have you come, Rafe? Why have you really come?"

It was time to reach a decision. His choices were clear. He could carry through with his original plan—extract a revenge that would put a fast end to any further Cinderella Balls. Or he could achieve the same result while satisfying the need burning between them. By his presence alone, a fire had been set. As he'd danced with her, the sparks had fallen to dry kindling. It wouldn't take much to fan it, one kiss and the flames would rage out of control.

From there he knew the progression well. Once the fire had been fed for a time, it would settle into a delicious, hot flame. Too bad it couldn't last, but such was the nature of fires. From hot flame it would slowly burn down, dying to warm embers before the inevitable fade to cold ashes.

The choice before him took little thought. The final outcome would be the same regardless—tonight would see the last Montague ball. As to how he went about it... His hungry gaze feasted on Ella. He'd be a fool if he didn't take that which would fall so easily to his grasp. She wished to marry. He could save her from such foolishness. And he could prove to her, as well as to her parents, that the Cinderella Ball was a dangerous illusion.

"Why have you come?" she repeated. "What do you want?"

His decision made, he tugged her into his arms. "I want a wife, *mi alma*. And you shall provide one for me."

CHAPTER TWO

ELLA stared at Rafe in disbelief. He was destroying her. Bit by bit, piece by piece he dimmed the light of hope she'd guarded with such care—the hope that she'd experience a love as eternal as the one her parents had found. Did he really expect her to provide him with a wife? How could he, after the past they'd shared? He must have some idea of the pain that would cause. Or was it that he didn't care?

She moistened her lips with the tip of her tongue, praying she'd misunderstood. "You can't be serious."

"I'm very serious." He continued to hold her in an embrace that made intelligent thought a sheer impossibility. The one time she attempted to pull free, his hand settled on her hip, anchoring her more firmly in the harbor between his thighs. "I want you to find me a woman."

"And how do you propose I do that?" Stress added a husky edge to her voice, but if Rafe heard he didn't let on. "Scurry from room to room, making an announcement?"

"Nothing that drastic," he replied in amusement. "I would think after all these years, you'd have some idea of how to go about it. Isn't the purpose of your Cinderella Ball to play matchmaker to a host of lonely individuals?"

"Well, yes. But—"

"Then be my personal matchmaker. How do the other guests find their mates?"

"I don't know." At his skeptical look, she insisted, "Really, I don't. I've never participated in the process."

He didn't take the hint. "You will tonight. Now answer my question. How is it done?"

"I suppose the guests introduce themselves to each other," she told him. "Most seem to have some preconceived notion of the sort of person they'd find compatible." She searched her memory of past balls. "Some even bring lists."

"A list? How...practical." His eyes glittered like raindrops on a windowpane. "Is that the way you intend to find a husband, by making a shopping list?"

"Not exactly." How had she gotten herself into this conversation? "I have certain qualities and characteristics I consider important—"

"That sounds like a list to me." When she started to contradict him, he added, "But if that's what it takes, who am I to argue? You have far more experience than I."

This was ridiculous! "Rafe, please—"

"No, no. We must do this right. If a list is necessary for a successful pursuit, than a list it is. What shall we choose as our first requirement?" He snapped his fingers, the retort as sharp as a hunter's rifle. "I know."

"She has to be of the female persuasion, right?" Ella interrupted, the glib remark escaping before she could prevent it.

His only response to her baiting was a slow smile. "Not just any female. She must be special, *amada*. Very special." His thumb swept the arch of her cheekbone and his voice softened, the faintest of accents giving his words a seductive lilt. "One with eyes like a desert sun."

Anger kindled as she fought to throw off the spell he wove with such skill. Did he think her without any feeling at all? He held her in an unbreakable hold, subverting her already fragile defenses with every look, word and touch until her emotions were in a state of total chaos. And then he had the unmitigated gall to describe the woman of his dreams in that calm, rational manner of his? A woman *she* was expected to find for him?

"Desert sunshine?" Ella questioned dryly. "You expect me to run around and see if any of the women here have hot eyes? That should make for an interesting evening."

His mouth twitched. "I have every confidence in your ability."

She released her breath in a silent sigh. Why did she bother goading him? She'd never won such a contest in the past. It seemed unlikely that she would now. "Is that it—a hot-eyed woman? Or is there more?"

His arms tightened a fraction, realigning her smooth curves to fuse with his sharper angles. "I have quite a few requirements. She should also be elegant and warm-hearted. She should have a bite to her, tempered with compassion for those less fortunate."

"This *is* a woman we're talking about?" Ella asked dubiously. "Because it's beginning to sound an awful lot like you should get yourself a dog, instead."

This time she did get a rise out of him. A hint of annoyance gave his reply a grating edge. "Your attitude isn't helpful," he informed her. "You wish to find a husband tonight, yes?"

"Yes." Maybe. After seeing Rafe again, she wasn't as certain as she'd been this afternoon.

"Until I find a wife, you won't be free to do so. Now, I suggest we get on with this."

Ella gritted her teeth. She'd love to tell him to go to hell. But she didn't dare ignore his earlier warning—that if she didn't cooperate he'd choose his own way of set-tling their differences. There was still time for her to find a husband, she tried to console herself. Not much, but some. All she had to do was locate the wife of Rafe's dreams. The woman had to be around here somewhere. Surely it wouldn't be *that* difficult to find her. Once Ella had unearthed this paragon for Rafe, she'd be free to give her heart to another. She bit down on her lip to keep it from trembling.

Assuming she had a heart left to give.

"You're right," she conceded. "Let's get this over with. What else do you want in a wife?"

"Let's see... She must be intelligent. And strong."

"So, you want a muscle-bound genius with the attributes of a dog." She offered a guileless smile. "Have I got it right?"

"*Amada*," he said dryly. "You're not getting into the spirit of things." He tilted his head to one side, fixing her with eyes capable of piercing clear to her soul. "Or don't you believe the Cinderella Ball can provide me with an appropriate woman? What's happened to your faith? Don't you believe anymore?"

"Of course I do!"

But his question had hit with pinpoint accuracy and she prayed that he didn't suspect the truth. Had he any idea how close she'd come to giving up? Did he know that she considered this her last chance to experience the magic of the Cinderella Ball?

"I still believe," she insisted, as though the mere act of speaking the words aloud would give them validity. "I do."

For a heart-stopping moment his eyes narrowed. Then he inclined his head. "I never doubted it." His hand crept upward, brushing the wispy curls from her temple. "Let's see... Where were we?"

He continued to hold her far too close, his touch making it more and more difficult to breathe normally, let alone respond in a natural fashion. "We were discussing the qualities you'd like in a wife," she prompted, fighting to conceal her distress.

"So we were. I wonder what else we should add to our list?" He paused to consider and his hand drifted from her temple to stroke the side of her throat. Supple fingers slipped beneath the sleek knot at the nape of her neck, sending a riot of sensations shivering through her.

She drew a short, panicked breath. "I think your list is long enough," she managed to say.

"You could be right." Humor rippled through his satiny voice. "Though I confess I have a preference for dark-haired women. You will keep that in mind, won't you?"

"I'll do my best. Anything else?" she demanded. His touch grew bolder, more provocative with every passing moment. If he didn't release her soon, she'd thoroughly disgrace herself by clinging to him and begging that he never let her go.

"I can think of just one more requirement."

She closed her eyes in a mixture of relief and regret. "Which is?"

His fingers played a tantalizing dance down the length of her spine to cup the curve of her hip. "When I kiss her, her response must be as abandoned as... This."

Before she realized what he intended, he lowered his head and captured her mouth with his. The heat simmered between them, then exploded, consuming her in a fire she had no hope of containing. An instant later she realized she didn't want to contain it. She wanted to feed the flames, burn higher and hotter and brighter until nothing mattered but the pleasure that could be gained from this timeless moment.

She caught his shirt in her hands, tugging him close, satisfied only when she could feel the swift, strong beat of his heart beneath her palms. His arms felt like corded steel, his hold as unrelenting as his nature. After all this time, she shouldn't still want him so desperately. She should resist, fight the trap he'd sprung. But the truth was, she'd been waiting for this to happen since he'd first appeared in the entranceway to the ballroom.

It had been so long since they'd last kissed. To her amazement, she discovered she hadn't forgotten a thing. Not his smooth, intoxicating flavor. Not the firm, warm feel of his mouth. Not the soul-jarring response of her body to his bold touch. She traced the tiny scar on the left side of his bottom lip knowing by his shiver that he found their embrace as affecting as did she. For a fleeting instant, it gave her hope.

"You understand now, don't you?" he whispered against her mouth. "This is how it should be between a man and woman. How can you think of giving yourself to another when you still burn like this for me?"

His words ripped into her heart. "What about that perfect woman you described in such detail? You may object to my plan, but you intend to marry a stranger tonight, too." Her regard turned caustic. "Or is it different for men?"

"For some men, perhaps."

He didn't say whether he was one of them or not. But the stark need in his gaze told its own story. He wouldn't be satisfied until he'd had her. The knowledge became a certainty, leaving behind a disconcerting bewilderment. There was only one way he could satisfy that desire. Only one way she'd consent to giving herself to him.

As though reading her thoughts, he said, "Yes, *amada*. I know the price I must pay to have you."

"But what about the woman you wanted me to find?" she demanded. "Remember? The hot-eyed brunette?"

His lids drifted downward, concealing the expression in eyes that had gone smoke-gray. "Ah, yes. Her."

"Yes. Her."

"Could you not tell?" When he looked up again it
was with a lazy amusement that sent time tumbling
backward. "It was you I described."

It took a full minute for his meaning to sink in. "I'm
the muscle-bound genius with the attributes of a—" She
couldn't say it.

He grinned. "Regrettably, yes. But I'm willing to be
generous and overlook such obvious failings."

Disbelief warred with an uncontrollable surge of hope.
"You can't be serious."

"Very serious. You wish to have a husband. I wish
for a wife. What could be more natural than we each
fulfill the other's desire?"

Ella felt as though she teetered on the brink of a
perilous abyss, that to believe in Rafe would be the same
as flinging herself over the edge into arms that might
fail to catch her. If she misjudged him, she'd end up
free-falling with nothing below to impede her plunging
descent. Nothing to catch her before she hit the unfor-
giving chasm floor.

Her composure slipped, revealing the vulnerability
beneath. "Are you asking..."

"I am asking you to marry me." His soft, persuasive
words filled the moonswept glade, adding to the magic
of the setting. "Marry me, Ella. You know it's what we
both want. What we've wanted for years. We can't look
at each other, touch each other, without being torn apart
by our need."

She shook her head. It wasn't possible. They couldn't
just start over. Not after all this time, not after the past
they'd shared. "You don't love me. You can't. Have you
forgotten—"

"I have forgotten nothing!" For an instant she caught
a glimpse of rekindled fury, of a man still thirsting for
vengeance. Then he visibly reined in his anger, banking
the blazing fire storm once more—at least, for the

moment. "What happened between us is in the past where it belongs. You must forget all that for a moment, Ella, and answer my question. Do you intend to marry tonight?"

"I'm considering it."

He captured her face in his hands, his work-roughened palms sparking a delicious friction along the length of her jaw. "Your expression gives you away," he warned. "However you choose to qualify your response now, your original plan was to marry. Admit it, Ella. Is that not true?"

"All right, yes!"

A dozen warring emotions swept across his countenance, too swift and confusing for her to follow, their passage like snowflakes driven by a savage winter wind. "Something has pressured you into taking such a desperate gamble. What is it?" he demanded.

In that instant her motivations crystallized and she hated him for forcing her to face the truth. For a split second she saw her decision through his eyes, recognizing the desperation that spurred her actions. Fear had driven her to take such drastic measures, not that she could admit that to him.

"I planned to fall in love this evening and marry," she evaded the question. "Just like my parents. Just like a thousand other couples who have found happiness at the Cinderella Ball. Is that so wrong?"

His fingers played a delicious melody across her bared shoulder. "But this can't happen, *mi alma*," he informed her gently. "For how can you go to another man when you have nothing to give him?"

She stared in confusion. "I don't understand. What do you mean?"

"Just what I said. You have nothing to offer this man. Do you not realize?" He paused for a devastating instant. "I still hold your heart."

"No!"

"You can't lie to me. Not after what we just shared. I know the truth."

How could she have given so much away with a single kiss? She couldn't bear it, couldn't stand to have him that intimately aware of her deepest most feelings. "Please let me go, Rafe," she begged, knowing the words were futile even as she uttered them. It was clear he'd already determined the path their future would take.

He had no intention of releasing her.

"I can't," he said, confirming her worst fears. "I can't allow you to marry another. It would be dishonest, the marriage a sham. He would come to hate you for it. You must realize that?"

Her throat closed over and she shook her head, incapable of speech.

"Listen to me," he insisted. "What exists between us is something neither of us planned. When I came here tonight, I didn't expect to look at you and feel what I do." Shadows carved his face into harsh, uncompromising lines. "Can you think otherwise?"

"No," she agreed tightly. "I'm sure you didn't attend the ball because you still had a romantic interest in me."

"Just as I can presume that when you decided to find someone of your own this evening, you believed what was between us had ended long ago." His wry expression acknowledged the vagaries of fate. "But it hasn't. It's still there."

Tears of defeat gathered in her eyes. She'd lost. She'd sworn she'd give the Cinderella Ball a final chance, that she'd give love a final chance. And in one devastating move, Rafe had stolen that possibility from her. "So what happens now?"

"It's quite simple. We take the same path all the other guests follow in a situation like ours. We marry."

He'd suggested as much before, but she still couldn't believe he was serious. Her hands tightened around the unyielding muscles of his arms. He was pure, indomitable strength, she a fragile barrier in his pathway. Still, she had to summon the fortitude to stop him, to prevent him from carelessly doing that which could not be later undone.

"No, Rafe. It wouldn't work."

"It would. It's practical. Logical. And I promise..." His mouth feathered across hers in a tantalizing caress. But even as he wrung a helpless response, his lips were gone, leaving her frustrated and unfulfilled. "I promise, you'll find our marriage quite satisfying."

She looked down so she wouldn't be swayed by the desire that turned his eyes to silver flames. She had to fight him, had to alter the course he'd set. "After all that's occurred in the past, how can you even suggest that we build a future together?"

"This is the Cinderella Ball. A night of fantasy and magic and miracles," he had the nerve to remind. "I thought that meant anything was possible."

"With another man, perhaps," she flung back. "But not with you. You don't believe in fantasy or magic, let alone miracles."

"I'm here, aren't I?"

"You didn't come because you wanted what the Cinderella Ball had to offer. You came here to cause trouble. Well, congratulations. You've succeeded."

He gathered her in his arms, tucking her head in the hollow of his shoulder. He'd held her like this more times than she could count. But never had it seemed so right, so natural. His touch felt more solicitous than provocative, the overt sexuality still there, though muted. And while his kiss had successfully destroyed most of her defenses, his tenderness reached far deeper, to the inner core she'd hoped he'd never breach.

"*Amada*, don't you understand that we have no choice? You may have wished to find a husband, but it wouldn't have worked. You say you believe in the magic tonight brings to special couples. Can you not believe that magic was meant for us, as well? Is it not possible that—regardless of what prompted me to come—the end result was preordained? We were meant to be together."

She lifted her head, forcing herself to reject what little comfort he offered. "If you were a different sort of man, I could believe such a thing could happen. I've always considered the Cinderella Ball capable of changing any man." She broke off, deciding for once to choose wisdom over valor.

A bleak emptiness settled over Rafe's rigid features, like winter over a barren plain. "Finish it," he ordered. "This night can change any man. Any man...except me?"

She looked at him unflinchingly, sorrow dimming the brilliance of her gaze. "Yes, Rafe. Except you. You're too hard. Too ruthless and self-contained. You don't trust anyone. You keep suspicion as your constant companion and hold all emotion at bay."

The first natural smile of the evening broke through his grim facade, the sheer beauty of it only adding to her misery. "But, you haven't mentioned any of my faults. There must be one or two you can think of."

"You see?" She attempted to lever herself off the brick wall of his chest. "What I consider negatives, you see as positives."

"A most fortunate circumstance." He tucked her back into the curve of his shoulder. "It'll bring balance to our relationship."

She gave up the struggle to win her freedom and relaxed against him. Her only hope was that sober reasoning would counter the intoxication of desire. "I'm serious about this, Rafe. You're a man without faith and

I haven't enough for the both of us. I couldn't bear the eventual outcome.''

He lifted an eyebrow. "And what outcome is that?"

"That once you'd satisfied your curiosity, you'd be furious with yourself—and with me—for allowing moonlit madness to overrule common sense."

"Curiosity?" Sudden anger rippled through him and his hand sought the swell of her breast, carefully palming its weight. "You think *this* is mere curiosity?" he countered. His gaze held hers as his thumb grazed the straining tip. "You can't be that innocent, *amada*."

The breath exploded from her lungs in short, uneven bursts. Heaven protect her, but his touch awakened a deep, helpless yearning. She fought for control, to conceal the torturous craving he'd stirred to life, a craving that stripped away the thin veneer of civilized behavior. She grasped his wrist, tugging futilely. She couldn't think when he touched her, and he knew it—knew it and used her defenselessness to emphasize his point.

"This isn't fair!" she protested. "I don't deny that I want you. How can I?"

A blistering fever raged deep in his eyes, one that matched her own. "You can't. It's as evident as my desire for you." He urged her tight within the cradle of his thighs to prove his point. "And it makes me just as vulnerable."

Ella gathered what remained of her inner resources. She had to stand firm. To give so much as an inch invited disaster. "That doesn't change the facts," she argued. "And the fact is that if we married you'd wake up one morning and realize that sex hasn't rid you of your anger. You'd feel trapped and you'd resent me. Little by little that resentment would grow until it consumed every aspect of our lives. Don't you understand? I couldn't live like that, waiting for the inevitable to happen. I think it would destroy me."

Tension radiated from him. "You see far too clearly," he whispered.

"Then you'll end this?" Emotion threatened to choke her, relief vying with disappointment. "You'll let me go?"

She could see the debate seething within, his face drawn taut from the effort. Slowly he shook his head, an air of implacability cloaking him. "If you had no feelings for me, I might consider it. Despite what you think, I couldn't force myself on you." He'd come to a decision, she realized, a decision she didn't have a hope of altering. "But that isn't the case."

"You would sacrifice our future for a momentary pleasure?" She tried one final time.

His expression turned fatalistic. "The moment is all we have. No one knows what tomorrow will bring. You predict only one possible future."

"The most likely one."

He didn't deny it. "I will not allow you to marry another," he replied instead.

His calm assertion infuriated her. "You won't allow...? How do you plan to stop me?"

"Suffice to say, I will prevent it."

"But, I have to marry tonight!" The words were out before she could stop them, revealing far too much by the passion they contained and by the depth of despair they reflected.

He stilled, fixing her with the full force of his attention. "Marrying tonight can't be that important."

This time she kept carefully silent.

His brows snapped together. "*Dios*! It is that important to you. Why, *amada*? Why is it so vital that you find a husband?"

"It's none of your business, Rafe. It stopped being your business a long time ago."

His anger dissipated, replaced by a tenderness that almost proved her undoing. "I regret to inform you... That has now changed."

"Don't do this to me, Rafe. Please."

"What is wrong?" he questioned gently. "Why this urgency to leap into marriage?"

"You wouldn't understand." She made a helpless gesture. "I just have to find a husband tonight and that's all there is to it."

"You *have* to?" A frown creased his brow and he caught her by the shoulders, holding her at arm's length. The lines bracketing his mouth deepened as his eagle-eyed gaze swept her from head to toe. "You are with child? You must find a father? Is that why you're so anxious to marry tonight?"

"No, of course not!"

His tension dissipated. "I'm relieved to hear it. A baby would complicate matters."

"Because you wouldn't want to raise another man's child?"

He shrugged philosophically. "By the time you gave birth, the baby would be ours, regardless of how it came to be conceived."

His casual acceptance of such a possibility caught her by surprise. "Then—"

"The complication arises from the problems that still exist between us," he explained patiently. "We have enough on our plate to deal with, don't you think?"

She couldn't deny it. "Rafe—"

"Enough, Ella. It's time to come to a decision. If you wish to acquire a husband this evening, there's only one possible solution. We will marry. If, on the other hand, you feel there is too much between us, then I'll walk away. I leave it up to you."

"And if I elect to marry someone else?"

His eyes darkened to a steely gray. "It won't happen."

It would be pointless to argue further. No matter how hard she fought to deny it, he was right. She couldn't bring herself to marry another. Not after seeing Rafe, being held and kissed by him. That just left one final determination.

Did she marry Rafe or commit herself to a life alone?

As though aware of the dilemma she faced, he released her and took a step backward. If he'd said it aloud, he couldn't have made his feelings any clearer. The choice was hers. He wouldn't try and sway her any more than he had already.

The surrounding darkness enclosed him in a tight embrace. She could still make out his silhouette, tall and lean and muscular. But his features remained shrouded, only his quicksilver eyes glittering from the black depths of the night. They held her with a steady calmness, already accepting her verdict.

If she refused him, he'd walk away and she knew with an instinctive certainty that she'd never see him again.

And if she accepted him? How would her life change? For it would change, there could be no question about that.

She closed her eyes. In the end all that mattered was vital fact. She loved Rafe, loved him with all her heart and soul. The Cinderella Ball had wrought its magic after all, offering her a final opportunity to discover "happily-ever-after." Now it was up to her to take advantage of that opportunity. She just had to reach out and accept what Rafe offered. Just reach out...

Slowly she opened her eyes, her decision made.

"Yes, Rafe," she whispered, extending her hand. "I'll marry you."

CHAPTER THREE

ONCE Ella had agreed to marry Rafe, he didn't give her a single second to reconsider. Perhaps he didn't dare. Sweeping from the shadows, he captured her hand and escorted her toward the bright lights of the house.

It was late, Ella realized in surprise, taking note of the almost deserted garden. Far later than she'd suspected. The crowd had thinned during the time she'd been secluded in the glade, until only a trickle of couples remained. She peeked at Rafe. Thank heavens he hadn't been serious about finding a wife among the guests. The choices would have been limited.

As limited as her choices for a husband, came the disconcerting thought.

"Where do we marry?" he questioned briskly, as they entered the dining room and skirted the buffet tables.

"We have to get a license first. There's a county clerk stationed in the library with the necessary applications." She cast a wistful glance at the wide selection of delicacies they bypassed. Nerves had prevented her from eating very much today and she was beginning to feel the effects. Perhaps she could nibble after they were married. She slanted another look at Rafe's set features.

Or perhaps not.

Rafe hesitated outside the dining room to get his bearings and then turned down the appropriate hallway. Opening the door to the library, he ushered her inside. They found the county clerk stationed behind a massive oak desk wearing a name tag that read, Dora Scott. In front of her she'd propped a sign that had originally announced, "For faster service, feed me hors d'oeuvres." But at some point during the evening, the word "don't" had been squeezed in as an afterthought and underscored twice in heavy black ink.

Rafe studied the sign and grinned. "*Don't* feed you hors d'oeuvres? You're certain?"

Dora returned his smile, falling for his charm as thoroughly as every other woman Ella had ever known. "Not if you want my help. That sign seemed like a brilliant idea at the beginning of the evening. But as the night's worn on, it's drifted from brilliant to uncomfortable to downright nauseating."

"Perhaps we could arrange for something to ease your problem," Rafe suggested. "Would that be acceptable?"

The clerk sighed in relief. "You take care of that for me and I'll have your forms processed in triple time."

"Done."

Rafe crossed to speak to one of the white and gold liveried attendants stationed in the hallway. While he made the arrangements, Dora whipped through her paperwork. By the time she'd finished, a small bottle of pink medicine rested at her elbow.

"You're a lifesaver," she told Rafe gratefully. She held out a blue and white envelope. "Give these forms to whomever officiates at your wedding ceremony. There's a souvenir certificate inside that you can keep. But it's not real. That comes later in the mail."

"Thanks for your help," Ella murmured.

Dora fixed her with a curious gaze. "You're the Montagues' daughter, aren't you?"

A flush mounted Ella's cheeks. "I guess the application I filled out makes it a dead giveaway, doesn't it? A name like mine has a tendency to stand out."

"It is rather unusual," Dora acknowledged with a sympathetic smile. "Will your parents be surprised when they discover you're getting married?"

Ella glanced uncertainly in Rafe's direction. "You could say that."

Shocked and horrified might be closer to the truth. When she'd agreed to marry, she hadn't taken their reaction into consideration. Now she wondered how on earth she'd explain it to them. But then...

Maybe it wouldn't be so difficult after all. They knew how she felt about Rafe. They had every confidence in the magic of the Cinderella Ball. And more than anything, they wanted her to be happy. Besides, it would only take three simple words to reassure them: *I love him.*

Once she'd told them that, their fears would be allayed.

"Well, good luck to you," Dora was saying. "I'll give you one piece of advice before you go, if you don't mind." She grinned. "Or even if you do mind."

"Which is?" Rafe asked.

"Do right by each other and you can't fail."

For a fleeting instant darkness shadowed Rafe's features. And then it was gone. "Sound advice," he said in an equitable tone. But the words sounded as short and clipped as exploding bullets.

"I thought so, or I wouldn't have offered it. Now go get married and let me polish off this pink stuff." Dora brightened. "If it works, maybe I can enjoy some more appetizers."

Laughing at her expression, Ella slipped a hand in Rafe's and left the library.

"Where do we go next?" he asked.

She hesitated, her brows drawing together in response to the terse nature of his question. What had happened to upset him? she wondered in dismay. He'd been fine until... Until Dora had advised that they do right by each other. Would that advice be so difficult to take? Did the memory of past events still stir his anger?

Did he still blame her for what had happened to Shayne?

"We go upstairs," she finally said. "The wedding ceremonies are conducted in the salons off the ballroom." She slowed her steps, forcing him to slow down, as well. "Rafe, we don't have to go through with this. No one is forcing us to marry. If you need more time to consider, I won't be upset."

"We're getting married. Now." He indicated an archway. "Through here?"

"Yes," she confirmed, realizing the futility of any further discussion.

He didn't speak again until they'd reached the appropriate rooms and even then it was only to say, "We appear to have a choice of services."

"Any kind you'd like. We'd hoped to make the occasion as special as possible by offering a full selection, something the couples would remember for the rest of their lives."

"I imagine it would be difficult for them to forget," he murmured. "Let's try this room."

He thrust open the first door and stepped inside. Ella followed, her breath catching in dismay. It was the "blue room," an elegant, rather formal parlor filled with dried flower displays, walnut end tables and blue silk-covered furniture. In front of the drawn drapes stood a podium behind which a justice of the peace conducted a generic wedding ceremony.

Rafe shot her a quick look. "What is it?"

Was she that easy to read? "Nothing," she insisted with a shrug.

He muttered a nasty-sounding word in Spanish, something she suspected she was better off not understanding. "I don't believe you, Ella," he stated flatly. "Tell me what bothers you."

"It's just..." She released a tiny sigh. "It's just that whenever my Great Aunt Mavis visited, we'd all come in here to talk."

"It brings back uncomfortable memories?"

"Only because I had to be so...*good*."

His expression lightened unexpectedly. "I can see where that must have been a strain."

She made a small face. "Don't laugh. I had to sit on the edge of that couch with my back straight, my hands folded in my lap and my ankles crossed for hours on end. Talk about torture! You try doing that at five years of age."

"At five I was hunting jaguar with my friends in the jungles of Costa Rica."

Shock held her rigid. "Your parents allowed you to do that?"

"There was only my father. My mother had died a number of years earlier and he hadn't yet remarried."

She glanced at him, curious. "I remember Shayne mentioning them. Your father came from Texas, didn't he?"

"A Texan with French grandparents. An interesting combination, don't you think? My mother was half Tico—Costa Rican. I've always suspected that my father escaped from his former life by marrying her. All I know for certain is that he didn't give a damn about anything, except growing coffee."

"That's why Spanish is your first language, isn't it?" she guessed shrewdly.

He shrugged. "It was the predominate language spoken." Before she could ask any more questions, he drew her from the room. "Since this place has such bad memories, we'll go elsewhere."

He opened the door to the next salon and Ella stared in disbelief. "When did my parents do this?" she marveled, crossing the threshold. "It's like we've stepped into a different era."

"Do you like it?"

"It's beautiful."

And it was. Huge wrought-iron holders stood in all four corners of the room, studded with thick white candles. Heavy chains held a chandelier made from a wooden wheel hub suspended from the ceiling. The only lighting in the room came from the massive stone fireplace and the countless candles scattered atop every available surface. They walked further into the room, the wide oak-pegged flooring echoing with each step they took. Between the tapestries hanging from the wall and the weaponry mounted above the mantel, it felt as though they'd wandered into a scene from the Middle Ages.

A minister rose from his seat by the stone hearth, the lenses of his wire-rim glasses reflecting the firelight. "Good evening and welcome. Would you like to be married?"

To Ella's relief, the tension faded from Rafe's face. Whatever concerns had plagued him earlier had apparently been laid to rest. "Yes, we would," he replied. "But we need a minute first." Not waiting for a response, he drew her off to one side.

"Is there something wrong?" she asked.

"You know what's wrong, *amada*. We can't marry like this. You'd always regret it."

She hardly dared ask. "My parents?"

"They should be here," he confirmed. "Would you like to send someone to notify them?"

"You're certain you don't mind?"

"I don't approve of their decision to hold another Cinderella Ball after what happened last time. But they should be present when their only daughter marries."

Tears pricked her eyes. "Thank you, Rafe. I'll send for them right away."

He turned back to the minister and surrendered the envelope Dora Scott had given him. "We'll marry as soon as the Montagues arrive."

After sending the message, Ella came to stand at his side. "They should be here in just a few minutes."

The minister inclined his head. "Very well. Before we begin, I'm required to ask that you give careful consideration to what you're about to do." His gentle blue gaze held theirs with grave deliberation. "Marriage is a serious commitment, requiring serious thought and consideration. So while we wait for the Montagues, I ask that you face each other and look at your partner. Make sure that your choice is the right one."

Ella turned to Rafe, surprised by his stoic expression. He held perfectly still, his features carved into harsh lines, his eyes a dark, stormy gray. And he waited, as if braced for a blow. It was almost as though he expected her to change her mind. Which was ridiculous. She never would. She tilted her head to one side and studied him. Or perhaps he didn't fear her changing her mind so much as...

The truth struck with stunning force. He feared that standing in such a reverent setting, she'd finally see what lay behind the mask he held up to the world.

She almost laughed aloud. Didn't he realize? Didn't he suspect? She'd seen behind that mask long ago.

He was an intriguing combination of elements, his singular background laying the foundation for the diverse set of qualities that had forged him into a man. When it came to his half-sister, Shayne, she saw someone of compassion and integrity. A concerned brother who would do anything to protect the one he loved.

But she'd also seen the ruthless streak in him. She'd learned from hard experience that he prowled through life like a lone wolf, wary of his fellow man, constantly on the alert for threat or weakness. Few dared cross him and those who did paid a stiff penalty. The fact that he didn't forgive easily made their marriage all the more surprising. For to marry her he had to first come to terms with their past.

Still, that didn't change one small fact.

Six years ago she'd fallen in love with him, flaws and all, and nothing he had said or done since had altered that.

She offered Rafe a reassuring smile. "I know the sort of man you are and I'm still willing to marry you."

Rafe froze, his hands knotting into fists. If she'd slapped him full in the face, he couldn't have been more stunned. What the hell did she mean by that—she knew the sort of man he was? Did she suspect? Had she figured out his plan? If so, why would she still be willing to marry him? She couldn't be so foolish as to ignore the ramifications. Once married, he'd keep her only so long as their passion burned hot. He'd prove to her once and for all that happily-ever-after lasted for about *cinco minutos* and not a damned second longer.

Didn't she understand? What they felt was lust, no more.

He'd fought for five long years to weed this woman from his life. And like some sort of tenacious vine, she'd wrapped herself around his heart and soul and held on with a strength that baffled him. Vines like that were dangerous. They didn't allow for mobility. Their roots sank deep into the earth while their tendrils burrowed through brick, stone and mortar, crumbling any and all resistance.

Still, that didn't change one small fact.

He wanted her. It was wrong. He'd regret his actions one day, he didn't doubt that for a moment. And that he'd pay an eternal penalty for the crime he intended to commit he accepted as just and proper. But at least he'd have brought closure to their relationship. Bitterness burned like acid in his belly. Why bother with lies? He wanted revenge as badly as he wanted Ella. Through marriage, he'd get both. Only one thing troubled him.

Looking into her clear golden eyes, seeing the sweet dreams that sparkled within their depths, he realized that he couldn't exact that sort of revenge. For Shayne's sake, he had to bring a certain death to any future Cinderella Balls. But to destroy Ella in the process—

"We're here!" Henrietta bustled into the room, Donald following behind at a slower pace. She drew to an abrupt halt when she saw Rafe. "Oh, dear," she murmured faintly. "Mr. Beaumont! What a...what a surprise."

Rafe inclined his head. "Mrs. Montague."

"What are you doing here?" Donald demanded with far less civility.

Before Rafe could reply and end a situation fast becoming a farce, Ella stepped into the breach, catching his hand in hers. "He came for me. We're going to be married and he asked that you join us."

"*Amada*, perhaps this isn't such a—"

"*You* asked that we witness the ceremony?" Donald interrupted sharply. "Not my daughter?"

Rafe shrugged. "To exclude you would have made Ella...unhappy. And I prefer her wedding be a pleasant memory."

Donald didn't appear convinced, but Henrietta breathed a sigh of relief. "It's a dream come true," she exclaimed. "It's what I've prayed for with all my heart."

And just like that—completely counter to what Rafe had anticipated—the Montagues gave their full approval. He closed his eyes in exasperation as the two descended on Ella, sweeping her into their arms for tearful hugs and kisses. When they'd finished with her, they turned to him. Henrietta gave him a warm embrace before linking arms with her daughter and crossing to the far side of the room for a private conversation.

Donald offered his hand. "I'm relieved all this nonsense is over between us," he said gruffly. "You almost broke Ella's heart holding her responsible for Shayne's actions."

"I still hold her responsible," Rafe retorted. "Don't think this marriage changes my views on that. Nor have I changed my mind about the Cinderella Ball. I marry your daughter in spite of these objections."

Donald remained silent for a long moment, his steady gaze holding Rafe's. "I think I understand," he murmured at last. "You regard this marriage as a means to several ends, don't you?"

Montague's insight didn't come as a surprise. As foolishly blind as he might be about the Cinderella Ball, he was still an intelligent man, aware that a person's nature contained as many flaws as strong points. As clearly as he saw those positive aspects, he also saw the negative. Saw... and accepted?

"You understand?" Rafe emphasized, folding his arms across his chest. "All of it?"

Donald released his breath in a long sigh. "Yes, Mr. Beaumont. I'm afraid so. You wish to have my daughter as well as your revenge."

"That's more than your daughter knows. You realize that, don't you?"

"She's in love with you. She's also a woman who prefers to see only the good in people. She undoubtedly hopes the good in you will overcome your need for vengeance. I, on the other hand, am more realistic."

Rafe lifted an eyebrow. It would seem that Ella's father truly did discern his reasons for marrying. "How do you intend to use this knowledge?"

"Dad?" Ella interrupted uneasily, leaving her mother to join their conversation. "Is something wrong?"

Donald slid an arm around his daughter's shoulders and dropped a reassuring kiss on her brow. "Nothing at all. Just renewing my acquaintance with your husband-to-be. Sweetheart, would you mind sending for refreshments?"

"Champagne?" she suggested.

"That would be perfect." He waited until she'd moved out of earshot before continuing. "And to answer your question, Mr. Beaumont—"

"Rafe."

"If you prefer," Montague allowed. "What I plan to do is quite simple. I plan to celebrate my daughter's marriage."

"That's all?" Rafe frowned. "Now it is I who am confused. You will stand by and say nothing?"

Donald's regard held calm resignation. "Believe me, I understand what you hope to get out of this marriage. Whether you succeed or not is another story."

"Do you doubt it?" Incredulity laced his question.

"Yes, as a matter of fact I do," came the composed reply. "Because there's something you've neglected to take into consideration."

The older man's assurance gave Rafe pause. Had he forgotten some vital point, missed some minor detail that Montague had spotted? He swiftly analyzed every aspect of his plan, searching for the hidden flaw. His eyes narrowed. There was nothing he hadn't already anticipated.

Nevertheless, wisdom dictated he be certain. "What have I overlooked?"

"You've neglected to consider that the head doesn't always rule the heart. If it did, you wouldn't be marrying my daughter."

It took every ounce of restraint for Rafe to maintain his cool. Fury simmered through his veins, desperate for an outlet. "You're mistaken," he snapped. "I never allow emotion to influence my decisions."

Ella's father inclined his head. "In that case, I look forward to having this conversation again at the Anniversary Ball. By then we'll both know who's correct."

Rafe stiffened. "What Anniversary Ball?"

"I assumed you knew," Donald said in surprise. "One year from tonight all the guests who wed are invited to return to celebrate their first anniversary with us. It's a tradition."

In a lightning-swift move, Rafe pivoted to insure Ella didn't overhear their conversation. "Shayne?" he demanded softly. "She knew of this ball?"

Compassion darkened Donald's gaze. "I'm sorry, Rafe. She did."

"That's where she was going the night...?"

"I'm sorry," Montague repeated, regret and sincerity implicit in his voice. "If it's any consolation I swear to you that Ella didn't know of those plans. We heard about the accident after the fact, but decided not to tell her."

"I half expected Ella to call," Rafe admitted. "Not that I would have put her through to my sister."

"And Shayne? I heard she's recovered. How is she doing?"

"As well as can be expected." It wasn't a precise answer, but it was the best he could give.

"I hope you understand why we didn't tell Ella. It wouldn't have solved anything, only added to her burden." A hint of censure crept into his tone. "It's a burden she's carried for five years. Undeservedly so."

Rafe just stared at him. He felt cold, as cold as an arctic wasteland. When would he get it right? When would he save those in his care instead of destroying them? He couldn't stop his gaze from tangling with Ella's. She was a pure golden flame, promising to warm even the most frozen heart. His teeth clenched so hard his jaw ached. There was only one small problem. To warm a heart, there first had to be a heart.

"I cannot do this," he whispered.

"You can do it. And you *will* do it," Donald retorted in a forceful undertone. "Oh, don't look so shocked, my boy. I have my own reasons for wanting to see this marriage go through."

Rafe stared rigidly ahead. "Which are?"

"She wants you. Why, I can't say. But not once has her love faltered over the past five years. Can you claim as much?"

"You know my plans," Rafe said, ignoring the question. "So you must realize this marriage will not fulfill her dreams."

"That's a possibility—one I'll deal with *if* it happens."

"*When* it happens."

"Perhaps. Time will tell."

Rafe kept his gaze fixed on Ella. "Then so be it. You will accept the consequences of your inaction?" he queried in a stony voice.

"Just as you'll have to accept the consequences of your action."

Rafe inclined his head in acknowledgment and without another word, crossed to Ella's side. "You may begin," he informed the minister, capturing her hand in his.

The ceremony turned out to be relatively painless. The only glitch occurred when it came time to exchange rings. "I'm sorry, *amada*. I don't have a ring for you," Rafe confessed.

Ella nodded as though she'd anticipated as much. "You didn't plan to marry when you came here."

He refused to lie. "No."

"We have rings on hand," the minister offered. "You could use them until you're able to purchase the genuine article."

After a momentary hesitation, Ella shook her head. "If it's all the same to you, I'd rather not."

Reaching into the folds of her gown, she pulled out a thin golden rectangle—one of the tickets to the ball. The truth struck Rafe, as undeniable as it was painful. She held *his* ticket. Before she'd ever discovered the purpose of his visit, she'd stolen the gilded wafer from the basket as a keepsake.

He knew then what she intended to suggest, knew and wanted to shout a harsh refusal. But he couldn't. He couldn't be that cruel. For her sweet act left behind a crushing impression. No one had ever made such a romantic gesture before. Not for him. He fought a silent battle between a restless yearning for the impossible and bitter acceptance of the actual, struggling all the while to maintain an impassive front.

Heaven protect him from sentimental angels.

Ella warmed the ticket between her palms for a long minute then glanced at him. "Do you happen to have your pocketknife with you?"

"In my tux?"

His irony didn't divert her. She simply smiled. "If memory serves, you carry it everywhere."

Giving in without further protest, he reached into his jacket pocket and removed the folded knife. "Is there something I can help you with?" he asked politely.

Anticipation turned her eyes the color of sunlit honey. "Yes, please. Could you cut this ticket into two, one piece a little larger than the other?"

"And then?"

"I'm hoping they'll be malleable enough to roll into rings," she said with devastating simplicity.

A sharp pain twisted in the vicinity of his chest. "I'll see what I can do." He glanced at the minister and indicated the ballpoint pen lying on a nearby table. "Would you mind?"

"Please. Help yourself."

Unscrewing the pen, he removed the copper ink cartridge. His blade made short shrift of slicing the ticket in two, but the metal wasn't pliable enough to bend. Crossing to one of the candles scattered about the room, he utilized the scissor accessory on his knife to hold the smaller half of the ticket above the flame. In no time the metal had softened enough to mold. Using the thin ink cartridge as a guide, he rolled the ticket into a neat cylinder. A final twist curled it into a finger-sized circle.

"Perfect," Ella whispered in delight. "Now make the other half of the ticket into a wedding band for yourself."

He started to refuse, wanting to reject such a touching request. But looking into her face and seeing her anxious expression, stopped him cold. What did it matter if he wore a ring? Let her enjoy the moment, let her revel in all the small marital rituals, meaningless as they were. It wouldn't change the eventual outcome. It would only add greater impact to the lesson she'd soon learn.

Without a word, he fashioned the second ring and gave it to her. He couldn't bring himself to look at his bride as she placed it on his finger, though. His instinct for self-preservation was too strong for that. Instead he focused his full attention on the odd-looking ring. It burned into his finger like a brand. It must still be hot from the flame, he tried to tell himself, knowing all the while that it had cooled long ago or he'd never have allowed Ella to touch it.

As though from a distance he heard the minister impart the solemn vows. Heard a sweet, joyous voice repeat them, followed by another voice—one that was lower and rougher. Then the ceremony ended and it was no longer Ella Montague who stood by his side, but his wife.

Ella Beaumont.

"You may kiss the bride," the minister prompted with a smile, his bright blue eyes glittering from behind his glasses.

Rafe gathered his wife's face between his hands, intent on bringing a swift end to the ceremony. He had no problem with this part of the ritual. He'd have preferred a little more privacy, but he was patient. He could wait until they returned to his suite at the Grand to bring this night to its natural conclusion.

He lowered his head to deliver a swift, hard kiss. But instead of taking her mouth in a stamp of ownership, he found himself bestowing a kiss of infinite tenderness. She opened like a flower to the heat of the sun and like a hungry bee, he chased after her sweetness.

In that instant, he felt his control slip.

With a half-bitten exclamation, he released her and stepped back, furious with himself for letting down his guard for even so brief a moment.

Ella gazed at him in confusion. "Rafe?"

"My apologies, *amada*," he said roughly. "I got carried away. If you would say goodbye to your parents, we should go."

He silently endured another round of hugs and kisses, his tension mounting with each passing moment. If he didn't escape soon, he'd explode. He dragged air into his lungs, willing himself to hold on for the few remaining minutes before they could leave.

At the door, Donald offered his hand again. "I'll be interested to see which wins in this game you've started," he said as a farewell. "Your head or your heart."

Rafe flashed him a look of grim warning. "You would be foolish to bet on the heart."

"For my daughter's sake, I hope you're wrong."

"For your daughter's sake, you should hope I'm right," he growled in reply.

With that, he dropped a possessive arm around Ella's shoulders and swept her from the room.

CHAPTER FOUR

"THE SUITE is beautiful," Ella informed Rafe. She glanced at him from beneath her lashes, wondering for the umpteenth time if he'd begun to doubt the wisdom of their marriage. He'd barely spoken a word since they'd arrived at the Grand Hotel.

He didn't reply and she suspected he was so consumed by his own private demons that he hadn't heard her comment. Yanking at the bow tie constricting his throat, he prowled a sitting area that would have been spacious if not for his presence.

She crossed the room, joining him as he came to a restless halt in front of the floor-to-ceiling windows. The full moon had begun a slow descent, gilding the desert's stark features with silver. She turned from its cool beauty to confront the far starker features of the man beside her.

"What's wrong, Rafe?"

He rested his forearm against the plate-glass window and stared blindly at the surrounding landscape. "Your father puzzles me," he said at last.

She sighed in relief. So it wasn't their marriage that troubled him, but something her father had said. "I noticed you two were having a rather intense conversation before the wedding."

"I thought he would stop the ceremony," Rafe stated unexpectedly.

Nervous dread feathered a path along her spine. "Did you *hope* he would?"

"No."

"Then why—"

He swung around to confront her, folding his arms across his chest. He'd opened the top portion of his dress shirt and the soft cotton parted to reveal the bronzed skin beneath. A thin white scar sliced across the left side of his collarbone, snagging her attention. It hadn't been there five years ago.

Before she could ask about his injury, he said, "I thought he'd stop the ceremony in order to protect you."

She blinked in surprise. "Protect me? From what?"

His shoulders lifted in a casual shrug, but his eyes glittered darkly, seething with a desperate intensity. "Protect you from the man you planned to marry. Who else?"

Her gaze cut to the scar again and she frowned. "He knows as well as I that you'd never hurt me."

The bitterness of his laughter shocked her. "You don't honestly believe that, do you?"

She met his gaze with a calm assurance that came from the very bottom of her soul. "Did you marry me in order to hurt me?"

"I married you because I want you," came his oblique reply. He swallowed the distance between them, catching her arm in an iron grip. "I married you because it was the only way I could get you in my bed. The only way to keep you there until we'd had our fill of one another."

Her eyebrows shot upward. "Our fill? You mean making love is like quenching a thirst or—"

"Or sating a hunger," he interrupted forcefully. "Yes."

"I don't know about you, but a while after I've eaten I'm hungry again," she dared to tease.

"Don't mock me," he warned through gritted teeth. "Do you think I have never desired a woman before?

Do you think I have not taken her to my bed and—once satisfied—left without a backward glance?''

She tilted her head to one side. "No. As a matter of fact I don't believe that. The affair may have ended because you weren't right for each other, but you'd never just take what you wanted and then leave. Not without making sure she was satisfied, as well."

"Do not shape me into someone I am not!" His accent deepened. "It will make the truth that much harder to endure."

"What truth are you referring to? That once we've made love, that's it? It's all over?" She laughed, genuinely amused. "Do you think our feelings for each other are so superficial?"

"*Sí! No hay duda.*"

She wondered if he realized he'd answered in Spanish. Probably not. It only happened when he came under extreme duress. In fact, she'd only witnessed his losing control to that extent once before—which meant he considered this issue serious. Very serious.

"Did my father know you felt this way?" she asked. "Is that why he should have stopped the wedding?"

Rafe swung around, the edge of his fist hammering against the window casing. The glass shuddered beneath the impact. "He knew why I married you and still he stood by and did nothing. Why? Why would he do that?"

She thought carefully before answering. "Perhaps because he loved me and wanted what was best for me."

"No! That is not right." A muscle jerked in his cheek and he stabbed his index finger in the air to emphasize his point. "If he loved you, he would have dragged you from that room. He would have taken you as far from me as physically possible."

"But, why?"

"So I could not hurt you." He thrust a hand through his hair. "Don't you understand? He must make sure that no harm comes to you. It is his duty. His responsibility. Why does he shirk it?"

For some reason her father's actions—or rather, in-action—had infuriated Rafe. And though the reason for that fury eluded her, she felt an obligation to try and explain her father's point of view on the subject.

"You must realize that I'm a grown woman," she began.

His eyes flashed in dark amusement. "I have noticed."

"Then you must also realize that I make my own choices and my own decisions. Dad knows that, just as he knows that if my choices are wrong, I'll learn from them."

He made a sound of disgust. "Does he stand aside and allow you to wander into the path of an oncoming truck, confident in the knowledge that once it hits, you'll have learned not to make such a mistake again?" His sarcasm intensified. "Of course, you are injured beyond repair, but no doubt you have learned your lesson."

"Are you comparing yourself to a truck?" she asked. Despite his anger, a smile tugged at her mouth.

He set his jaw. "In this case, yes."

"It certainly makes for an intriguing image," she murmured. Not giving him an opportunity to vent a reply, she hastened to say, "Seriously, Rafe. My father will always be there to comfort me when I need it. But he can't wrap me in cotton wool in the hopes that I'll never injure myself. It would be pointless. He can't look after me every minute of every day. He can only do his best."

Rafe closed his eyes, visibly waging an inner war. She waited patiently until he looked at her again. The darkness had fled from his gaze, at least for the moment, and his eyes had turned from blackest slate to a brilliant silver-gray. He reached out and cupped her cheek, tracing her lower lip with the rough surface of his thumb.

"I could not do as your father has," he told her. "I could not stand aside while one I cared for was threatened."

"You're not a threat," she repeated.

His mouth twisted into a self-derisive smile. "And you, *amada*, are far too innocent. Too trusting."

"Because I believe in you?" She shook her head, her steady regard never wavering. "You're my husband. I'd trust you with my life."

A sigh shuddered from the depths of his chest. "Then heaven protect you, for I cannot."

"I don't need heaven's protection. All I need is you."

He drew her into his arms, the tenderness of his touch betraying far more about his true nature than he realized. Lowering his head, he rested his jaw against her temple. "Have you any idea what I have planned for you?" His words brushed the side of her face in a feather-light caress. "Do you?"

When had her ear become so sensitive? she wondered hazily. Or was it Rafe that made it so? "What have you planned?"

He nuzzled the side of her neck beneath her earlobe, warming the sensitive skin with his breath. "I plan to hold you in my arms while I strip away every scrap of your clothing."

A smile trembled on her lips. "How shocking. And then?"

"Then I'll carry you to the bed. And there I'll make you mine while the moon and stars look on."

"I see why you thought I needed protection," Ella whispered. "It sounds like a fate worse than death."

She slid her hands into the thick blackness of his hair and gave in to the temptation that had plagued her from the moment she'd set eyes on him. Pressing her mouth against the hollow of his throat, she tasted his unique flavor.

He tilted back his head to give her greater access. "Ah, *amada*," he muttered harshly. "I will regret this night. I will pay a thousandfold for what I do to you."

"Why such a steep price?" Hunger gave her voice a husky edge. "When it's what I want, too."

"Be very certain," he warned.

"I've never been more positive of anything in my entire life. Is that certain enough for you?"

He didn't need any further urging. The single shoulder strap of her Grecian-style gown parted beneath his hand and the bodice drifted to her waist, baring her. For a brief instant, a virginal fear kept her frozen in place. Then her breath escaped in a soft rush. This was Rafe, the man she'd wanted since she'd first learned what it meant to be a woman. She could no more fear him than she could fear the passing of night into day.

"*Dios*," he breathed. "I'm afraid to touch you. My control... It's shaky, *amada*. Very shaky."

"It's all right. I still trust you."

A near-silent groan spilled from his throat. "That may not be wise."

She stepped free of his embrace intent on proving her words with action. Reaching for the zip at the side of her gown, she tugged it downward. "According to you there's very little I've done this evening that's wise."

"Very little," he concurred, giving her every movement his strictest attention.

"And also according to you..." For a breathless moment the silk clung to her curves with nothing to hold it up but sheer defiance. He reached for her dress as though itching to lend gravity a helping hand. "... There's little I've done that's smart. Starting with our marriage."

"A bad decision." His graveled response betrayed how close to the edge she'd pushed him.

"And ending with this." Surrendering to the inevitable, her gown drifted to the floor like flaming fingers of gold.

His gaze could no more resist the pull of forces beyond his control than her dress. His breath hissed through his teeth as he looked his fill. "Ending? Oh no, *mi alma*, this is not an ending but a beginning."

"In that case..." She dropped her arms to her sides in a gesture of total faith. "I leave the rest to you."

"Your first wise decision." He reached for her, stopping mere inches from her breast. His hand quivered ever so slightly and with a muttered curse, he curled it into a fist. "I am but a schoolboy around you. Thank heaven I did not know how little lay beneath this dress."

"Or?"

He didn't evade the truth, but looked her square in the eye. "Or we would have been further delayed in that glade tonight."

"I'm not sure I would have minded."

His mouth tightened. "It would not have mattered if you had," he replied in a clipped, strongly accented voice. "I realize it does not speak well of my self-control. But to have seen you like this and left you untouched..." He shook his head. "It would not have happened."

He opened his hand again. This time his fingers were rock-steady. And when he reached for her, he didn't draw back as before. His eyes contained the silver flash and sizzling heat of summer lightning, his desire like a ferocious storm drawing her into its fiery center. Now it was her turn to tremble, for her thoughts to twist and scatter like leaves in the midst of an autumn gale.

At his first velvety caress, a startled cry escaped before she could prevent it. "Easy," he murmured. "You set the pace. I won't push faster than makes you comfortable. Tell me what you want. Tell me, *esposa*."

She knew that word, considered it the most beautiful she'd ever heard. *Wife*. "Kiss me, Rafe." She wrapped her arms around his neck. "Just kiss me and I'll know it's all right."

He sank his fingers deep into her hair, pulling the ebony curls free of its elegant knot. "A kiss to make you feel better about what's to happen this night?" he demanded. The silken strands spilled through his open hand like a midnight tide, swirling around her pale shoulders. "Is that what you want from me?"

Did he think her a child in need of reassurance? "No, not a kiss like that," she corrected unsteadily, her mouth teasing the tension from his jawline. "I want the sort of kiss a husband gives his wife on their wedding night. For the first time in my life, I want to experience a lover's kiss. A beginning without end."

The air seeped from his lungs. But instead of his tension easing beneath her tender caress, it increased, communicating itself to her in the tautness of his arms and the heavy beat of his heart. "*Mi amada y mi alma*," he whispered the husky words. "*Te adoro*."

Then slowly, powerfully, he cupped her bottom in his calloused hands and lifted her against him. Her breasts slid along the soft cotton of his shirt, the friction a delicious torture. It was incredibly erotic, her near-nudity a shocking contrast to his formal attire. For a breathless moment his hot silver gaze lay claim before his mouth captured hers. He held nothing back, rejecting the preliminaries to invade the warm interior, taking her with the desperation of a man too long denied.

Her hunger rose to match his, boundless in its need. She put every last bit of her heart and soul into the kiss they shared, saying with hands and mouth what he'd have rejected if she'd dared to speak aloud. She loved him. Dear heaven, how she loved him.

He released her mouth, seizing her lower lip between his teeth in a brief hungry bite. "Is that the sort of kiss you wanted?"

"It's a start."

She didn't know where she found the presence of mind to goad him. But it had an extraordinary effect. He reacted to the challenge with the swiftness of a hawk swooping toward its prey. He swept the legs out from under her, lifting her high in his arms. A few rapid strides carried them from the sitting room to the bed. Her high-heeled sandals thudded to the floor at the same instant as her backside hit the mattress. She bounced once before tumbling against the pillows.

He stood over her, his chest heaving beneath his gaping shirt. His eyes burned with an ardent promise that fueled her own painful need. "I've waited an eternity for this. But no longer."

Without a further word, he jerked the gold cufflinks from their holes and dropped them unheeded to the carpet. His shirt and cummerbund followed. And that's when she saw them—a dozen silver scars striping his chest and shoulders. With a shocked gasp, she bounded from the bed and flew into his arms. Now it was her turn to touch him with a shaking hand.

"Oh, Rafe," she murmured sorrowfully, tracing each jagged line with a gentle finger. "What in the world happened to you? Were you in an accident?"

"No."

"But—"

"I witnessed a car crash."

It took a split second to understand. Her gaze shot to his. "Dear heaven. You received these pulling someone from a wreck, didn't you?"

He gathered her close, catching her mouth in a soothing kiss. "Don't give me too much credit. It was Shayne trapped in that wreck. I feared the car would catch fire. If it had been a stranger..." He shrugged. "I may have had second thoughts about lending assistance."

Tears leapt to her eyes. "I know you too well to believe that. You would have helped no matter what," she disputed unevenly. "And Shayne? Is she all right? Was she badly hurt?"

"She has scars as I do, but she's recovered for the most part."

"I'm sorry. So sorry. I didn't know or I would have gone to see her." Ella pressed her lips to the thin white line that ran the length of his collarbone. "It terrifies me to think how fragile our lives are. How brief a time we have and how suddenly it can all end."

Rafe inhaled the sweet feminine fragrance of her hair and skin. The scent intoxicated him, eclipsed every thought but one. "Then we shouldn't waste another minute."

Palming her breasts, he paid reverent homage with his tongue and teeth to the delicate peach-tinted tips. They peaked sharply in response, pearling from the pull of his mouth. It wasn't enough. He wanted more of her. He wanted all of her. He slid downward, warming her belly with his breath as he stripped her of the final lacy bits of underwear. He smoothed the taut skin of her thighs and buttocks, feeling the supple muscles quiver in response.

"Rafe, please! I need you."

Gently, he slipped his fingers into the very heart of her. Her soft cry broke above him, shivering like frost-tipped leaves. She was all liquid warmth, a devastating combination of passionate purity and demanding sensuality. It wouldn't take much to push her over the edge, to feel her flame to life within his hands. Already her breath had grown shallow and rapid, an exquisite tension building beneath each stroking touch.

He released her, lifting her onto the bedspread, silk on silk. She looked at him, her eyes the color of molten gold, her need a silent cry. "Soon, *amada*," he soothed. "Very soon."

His gaze never left her as he swiftly stripped. She stiffened as he shed the last of his clothing, vulnerable in her innocence, strong in the power of her femininity. Finally he came to her, gathering her close. Passion rode him hard, threatening to break what little remained of his patience. He wanted to go easy with her. He wanted to be the honorable man she thought him, instead of the vengeful one he was. Just this once, he wanted to fulfill her dreams before she awoke to the brutal harshness of reality.

"Don't be afraid," he whispered. "I'll try not to hurt you."

"I'm not afraid." She cupped his face and he sensed she was gathering the nerve to speak. "I know you don't want my love... But you have it anyway. When I give you my body, I also give you my heart."

Words of rejection leapt to his tongue. He didn't want to hear this. Not now. Not if he had a hope in hell of finishing what he'd started this night. "Don't—" he began.

She sealed his lips with her fingers. "Please don't stop me. What I have to say is long overdue. You have no idea what it's been like these past five years. I thought I'd lost you forever. I thought I'd never have the opportunity to tell you what's in my heart."

He tried again, catching her wrist and dragging her hand from his mouth. "Some things are best left unsaid. This is one of them."

"No, it isn't. I love you," she repeated in soft wonder. "Don't you understand what a miracle that is?"

He turned his head, rejecting the slice of heaven she offered with such unstinting generosity. "It's no miracle."

"But it is." She laughed, the sound a silvery ripple. "You see, tonight was my last chance to discover that miracle. You didn't know that, did you?"

He tensed, swinging back to look at her. "What do you mean?"

"I mean that tonight was my last chance to experience the magic of the Cinderella Ball."

"Why?" He heaved himself onto an elbow, gazing down at her with all the hostility of a caged jaguar. "Why do you say that?"

"Over the past few years..." She gave a self-conscious shrug. "I'd begun to lose faith."

She couldn't mean what he thought. It would be too bitterly ironic. "Lose faith, how?"

"It must seem odd coming from me of all people, but... I'd almost stopped believing in the Cinderella Ball," she confessed hesitantly. "I'd almost stopped believing in magic and miracles and everlasting love. So, I decided to give it one last night in order to determine if those things really exist."

"This night? This was your last night?" At her nod, he demanded, "What if you didn't find love?"

"I made myself a promise. If I wasn't wed come morning, then I'd give up. I'd have proven that I was never meant to find happily-ever-after, that I wasn't one of the special people destined to receive the miracle of love." She traced the tense curve of his cheek, her eyes shining like golden stardust. "And then you walked in."

He shook his head in fierce denial of her words. "No."

"Oh, Rafe. Don't you see? It was fated."

"Ill-fated, you mean."

"No!" Her full mouth tilted in a tremulous smile. "You restored my faith. If you hadn't come tonight, I would have given up. I know I would have. And then I'd have realized you were right about the Cinderella Balls."

"I am right about them, Ella," he told her forcefully. "They're just foolish pipe dreams for desperate people."

"You're wrong, Rafe. You must see that now. If it hadn't been for you, I'd have spent the entire evening searching for a man to love. But it wouldn't have worked. I'd never have found him."

She was destroying him, inch by agonizing inch. "You don't know what you're saying."

"Yes, I do. You warned that I had nothing to offer anyone else and it's true." She clung to him, pressing close, the softness of her breasts branding his arm. "You have it all—my heart, my love, my future. It's all in your keeping."

"*Basta*!" He thrust her away and in one swift motion rolled to the side of the bed. He sat on the edge, the broad expanse of his back turned toward her.

"Rafe, what is it? What's wrong?" She scooted closer, laying a cool hand against his fevered skin.

"Don't touch me!" He tossed the curt words over his shoulder. "If you have so much as an ounce of self-preservation, you will not touch me."

The final rays of a dying moon cut a harsh path across his bowed head, catching in the deep crevices marking his face. He gulped air, his chest heaving beneath the effort. His muscles stood in high relief, corded into taut mountain ridges, as though he fought to sustain an unbearable weight.

"Rafe, what is it?" she whispered in concern.

His throat moved convulsively and his hand fisted on his knee. "Just give me a moment to regain my control." Drawing on battered inner reserves, he stood. In one swift motion, he snatched the silk comforter from the bottom of the bed and tossed it at her. "Cover yourself," he ordered.

She caught it automatically, wrapping herself in its concealing folds. "Please tell me what's wrong." Fear wove a shaky path through her words. "What have I done?"

"I can't go through with this," he replied, deciding to give her the truth, straight and unvarnished. "I thought I could, but I was wrong."

"You can't do what?"

He turned on her, thoroughly disgusted with himself but also irrationally furious with her for being so naive and trusting. When would she realize he didn't deserve her trust, let alone any of the finer emotions with which she'd gifted him?

"Why the hell do you think I married you?"

"You've told me that already. Because you want me." She held out a hand in appeal. "I know you believe it's only a physical attraction, but I think that given time—"

"Time will not change anything," he cut in, determined to end this farce. "Nor does it explain my presence at your home this evening. Perhaps you would care to guess my reasons for that?"

She groped for a response. "To... to resolve our differences," she offered tentatively.

"No, Mrs. Beaumont. Try again."

He waited, holding her gaze with an implacability she couldn't escape. He steeled himself to watch the comprehension dawn, to watch as disillusionment drained the animation from her delicate features. It didn't take long.

"Rafe, please. Don't do this."

"Answer me," he commanded. He kept his emotions rigidly in check, refusing to be swayed by the tiny spark of hope still reflected in her expression. "Why did I come this evening?"

The light of hope faded. "You came to get revenge," she whispered painfully.

"That's what has driven me all these years," he confirmed. "But my main purpose for attending tonight was to put an end to the Cinderella Balls."

Her chin lifted with the first hint of angry defiance. "By marrying me? How would that have ended the balls?"

He didn't answer. He couldn't. He couldn't put into words the plan he'd devised nor the manner in which he intended to execute it. She remained silent for several long minutes, lost in thought. Then once again comprehension dawned and he strove not to flinch as her face turned ashen.

"You..." She moistened her lips with the tip of her tongue. "You thought once we'd made love our feelings for each other would die. And that when they died, so would our marriage."

"I see you understand now."

"No," she whispered, shaking her head. "You're wrong. That's not what would have happened."

"We will have to disagree on that point," he said gently.

"You're serious?" She hugged the comforter tighter against her breasts. "You were going to make love to me and then leave?"

"Not quite. I wanted you more than one night's worth," he confessed with brutal candor. "A month or two would have seen the job done. By then you'd have realized that marriage isn't the miracle of love you seem to think. And you'd have run home to Mommy and Daddy a disillusioned but wiser woman."

"You believed my parents would have been so upset by my failed marriage, so disillusioned themselves, that they'd have stopped the balls?'' she questioned in disbelief. ''Well, I have news for you—''

He cocked an eyebrow. ''It wouldn't have worked? *No problema, amada*. I still have an alternate plan should they prove stubborn.''

She seemed to hesitate, as though compelled to speak, but deciding at the last minute to remain silent. ''You're referring to one of those alternatives you mentioned earlier in the glade?''

''*Qué coqueta*. But then you always were clever— when you weren't allowing your emotions to interfere with your reason. I've hesitated to take such drastic measures,'' he felt compelled to add. ''But make no mistake. I will end these balls.''

''Because of Shayne?''

His control broke and he caught her arm, yanking her close. ''Yes, because of Shayne! I'd do anything. *Anything*,'' he stressed, ''to protect others from her fate. You don't understand, do you? But then, how could you? You live a life of illusion. Nothing about your existence is real.''

She twisted free of his grasp, scooting toward the center of the massive bed. ''That's not true!''

''No? When you return to your fairy tale existence, *princesa*, open your eyes and take a good look around. Your cupcake castle has so many rooms even you are unfamiliar with them all. It sits in the midst of a desert and yet is filled with plants and shrubs better suited to tropical climes. I doubt they could survive without the protection of a fleet of gardeners and enough water to quench a small city. You hide from strife in a private glade with verdant sod to comfort your dainty feet and leafy trees to shade your fair skin. Well, real life isn't like that.'' His voice reflected his contempt. ''Ask Shayne.''

Tears glittered in Ella's eyes, tears she fought valiantly to conceal. "You still haven't answered my question. What happens now?"

"If I have a written guarantee from your parents that the balls end, nothing happens. You go home and the marriage is annulled."

"And if they don't agree?"

"If they refuse they will soon find themselves without the financial ability to throw another Cinderella Ball. And I warn you, it is well within my powers to do as I threaten."

Shock held her rigid. "That's what you came tonight to tell us?"

He didn't bother to wrap it up in pretty paper. "Yes."

"And then you decided—"

"That I still wanted you," he replied, determined to be blunt and brutal to the bitter end. "To my surprise, I discovered that you also wanted me. Our marriage was an alternate means to a similar end."

"While at the same time satisfying our...mutual desire."

"Exactly."

"So why didn't you go through with it?"

He gazed into her brilliant golden eyes. They gleamed like the last few rays of sunlight, fighting against the relentless push of night. He basked in those final moments of warmth, knowing it would never again be his. He gathered his strength. It was time to finish what he'd started.

"I discovered that revenge is not as sweet as I thought. In fact, it tastes quite bitter." He gave a careless shrug. "Besides, my point has been made. You spout sentimental nonsense about true love, about the magic of this inane ball. But you didn't find love or magic or a Prince Charming this evening, have you my *pobrecita* Cinderella? You found vengeance."

She didn't look at him, but remained crouched in the center of the bed, clinging to the comforter as though to a lifeline. "You're going to leave now," she said at last.

It wasn't a question.

"It would be pointless to stay." It took every ounce of control not to drag her into his arms, to set right this terrible wrong he'd done. Instead he retrieved his clothing from the floor and dressed. "I will give you time to reach your decision about future Cinderella Balls," he said as he gathered his belongings. "But I suggest that you not wait too long before reaching that decision."

"No," she whispered. "I won't wait too long."

"The room is yours until morning. There's no hurry to vacate."

"Thank you," she responded, unnervingly polite.

Rafe found the five minutes it took him to complete his packing more agonizing than any of the injuries he'd received rescuing Shayne. He almost wished the harm he'd caused could take on physical expression. Wounds that did not kill eventually healed. But in his heart of hearts, he knew that fate had no intention of being so kind. He'd bear these scars the rest of his life.

At the door, he turned and looked at Ella and his pain surpassed anything he'd ever felt before.

The golden sunshine had fled her gaze and the blackness of night consumed her.

And in that moment, the gates of hell opened to welcome him.

CHAPTER FIVE

"HE's not coming, is he?" Ella asked quietly as her father approached from the direction of the house.

She stood in the middle of the glade—the one Rafe had described in such caustic terms—and gazed at the moon. It would be full in another week, the second full moon since the Cinderella Ball. And it would offer yet another painful reminder of that disastrous night. Silvery light caressed her upturned face. Was Rafe in Costa Rica, also staring at a midnight sky? The thought caused her throat to close.

"No, my dear. He isn't coming back," Donald finally replied. He didn't offer his sympathy and she was grateful for his restraint.

"I'd hoped—" She broke off, bowing her head.

She'd hoped that Christmas might bring with it the miracle she'd prayed for with every fiber of her being. But just moments ago the huge grandfather clock in the hallway had laid that fantasy to rest. On the final stroke of midnight, Christmas Day had passed without a word from Rafe.

"No matter how it might look, he cares for you," her father insisted. "There's no doubt in my mind."

"What makes you say that?" She turned to confront him. "Do you think he cares because he called you the night we married? You'll have to excuse me if I don't find that a very convincing argument."

Donald sighed, the sound like the tired creak of a pine. "When Rafe phoned from the Grand's lobby, I'd never heard a man more tortured. He didn't just ask me to interrupt the ball and bring you home. He ordered me to.'' Her father dropped a hand to her shoulder, squeezing gently. ''If I hadn't done as he'd demanded, I suspect he'd have come after me personally.''

''I doubt that.'' Her laughter sounded shaky and she broke off, aware that it revealed far too much of her inner turmoil. ''He was well on his way to Costa Rica by the time you arrived.''

''No, Ella. He wasn't.''

Her head jerked up. ''What do you mean?''

''I doubt it would have made any difference if I'd told you two months ago.'' He hesitated for a brief moment. ''But perhaps it will now.''

''Told me what?''

''When I arrived at the Grand Hotel, I saw Rafe sitting in a cab outside. Just sitting and waiting while he smoked a cigarette. Waiting for me to come for you, I suppose.''

She shook her head. ''You must have seen someone who resembled Rafe. It couldn't have been him. He doesn't smoke.''

''He did that night. I saw him quite clearly.''

''What are you saying, Dad?''

''Just this... If ever a man needed his faith restored, it's Rafe Beaumont.''

''You're mistaken,'' she said with a slight smile. It amazed her that she could still find anything humorous about her husband. ''He doesn't want his faith restored. He doesn't even believe in such a thing. Just like he doesn't believe in magic or miracles or love.''

''Oh, he believes. That's why he fights so hard to deny it. You see, to believe in the untouchable, one must give up control.''

She frowned. ''I don't understand. What do you mean?''

"Rafe is a man who briefly lost control of his life a long time ago. When he regained that control, he swore never to lose it again."

"When was this?" she asked in confusion. "He never mentioned—"

"I'm not surprised. Perhaps someday he will. In the meantime, what you need to understand is that love... Well, when you love someone, you gift her with your heart and your body, even your soul. You are forever connected to that person, and therefore vulnerable. You can't control what that person may choose to do with your gift." He smiled, a sad, wise smile. "You've discovered that for yourself, haven't you?"

The first hint of hope dawned in her gaze. "You think Rafe loves me, don't you? But he denies it because it would mean giving up control."

"I can't answer that," Donald admitted. "Only he can. But I do believe he needs you. And I think you may be the only one capable of reaching him." He lifted a snowy eyebrow. "If that's what you want."

It didn't take any thought. "It's what I want," she said without hesitation.

Her father smiled, giving her a quick hug. "In that case, you have a suitcase to pack and a flight to schedule."

She gazed at him in wonder. "Yes, I believe I do."

Rafe stood outside, staring up through the tropical foliage at a midnight moon. His thoughts were consumed by Ella. Always by Ella. He took a deep drag on his cigarette, cursing himself for a fool. "I wish you'd put that thing out," Shayne said, approaching from the direction of the house. "It's going to ruin your health."

He shrugged. "Death is inevitable."

"Maybe so," she said, linking arms with him. "But you don't need to hasten its arrival."

He dropped his cigarette butt to the ground and extinguished it beneath his boot heel. "What keeps you up so late, *hermanita*?"

"I'm worried about you. You've been so...distant. So closed in. And I wondered if it might not have something to do with this." She caught his hand in hers, running a finger over the crude wedding ring he still wore. "You've never explained its presence, you know."

"There's nothing to explain."

"But you're married, aren't you?"

He hesitated briefly before giving a curt nod. "It need not concern you. The marriage is a temporary measure."

"Your ring has a familiar design." She glanced at him from beneath her lashes. When he kept stubbornly silent, she prompted, "It's made from a ticket to the Cinderella Ball, isn't it? My ticket?"

He didn't bother with pointless denials. "Yes, it's yours."

"And who wears the other?" When he didn't answer, she closed her eyes. Moments later her breath caught. "Oh, dear heavens. You married Ella, didn't you?"

"As I have said, this does not involve you," he said quietly. "All that matters is that I have put an end to them, Shayne. Soon there will be no more balls to tempt you."

"I don't care about the balls. I care about Ella. How could you?" she demanded. "How could you do that to her?"

"There was no other option." He thrust a hand into his pocket, dragging free the crumpled pack of cigarettes. Only one remained. He lit it, drawing the acrid smoke deep into his lungs. "I married her. And I left her. I took with me her hope and her dreams and left behind pain and despair." He tilted his head to one side, his expression colder than the icy peaks of Mt. Everest. "It was a fair exchange, don't you think?"

"Why, Rafe?" Shayne unhooked her arm from his and swiveled to face him. "Was it really necessary to hurt her?"

"It was the only way."

"But to hurt Ella, of all people." For the first time in years, he saw temper flash in her dark, liquid gaze. "I think I hate you for that, Rafe." Without another word, she turned and stormed back to the house.

"It's all right, *mi pequeña*." He lifted the cigarette to his mouth and drew an uneven breath. "I would expect no less."

Early in the afternoon of New Year's Day, Ella pushed open the door exiting the Juan Santamaría International Airport in Costa Rica. Instantly, she found herself surrounded by a pack of young boys.

"Carry your bags, *Señora*?" the first asked, hefting a piece of her luggage.

"You need Tico money?" requested the next.

"Taxi?" offered still another.

She glanced from one eager face to the next and smiled. "Yes, please."

Two of the boys peeled off, scurrying to take care of her needs. The third gathered the rest of her bags. "You come this way," he urged.

"Perhaps I should help you—"

He shot her a look of such indignation, she murmured a quick apology. "Come, *Señora*," he repeated, jerking his chin in the direction of the curb.

She followed, feeling guilty at allowing a child barely ten years old to carry so much luggage. But glancing down the sidewalk, she realized it seemed to be the practice here. School-age children littered the area, all offering their assistance to arriving tourists.

Bright sunlight assaulted her eyes and she slipped on a pair of sunglasses and jammed a floppy straw hat onto her head. After living for so many years in Nevada, protecting her eyes and skin had become a habit.

"I need to take a cab or a bus to the town of..." She pulled a copy of Rafe's marriage application from her purse and swiftly scanned it for the information she needed. "I need to get to the town of Milagro. Do you know where that is?"

"*Sí.*" He raised his voice, signaling to one of the boys who'd initially greeted her. "Diego! *Ve, trae a* Marvin."

The boy who'd offered to exchange her money returned just then with a young man in his early twenties. "You wish to buy Tico money, *Señora*?" the latest arrival asked.

Tico, she remembered Rafe explaining, meant Costa Rican. "Oh, yes. Please."

The transaction went smoothly, although she couldn't help wondering if Rafe would consider it a foolish risk to use a moneychanger instead of a bank. No doubt she'd find out when next they spoke. By the time she'd tucked the "*colones*" into her wallet, Diego showed up with the taxi driver in tow.

"Marvin, he take you to Milagro," Diego said.

A wide grin split the cabbie's face. "*Sí, no problema.* I live in Milagro." He signaled the boys to load her luggage into the trunk of his dusty orange cab. "I get you there very fast."

"Thanks. I'd appreciate that."

Tipping each of the boys who'd helped her—far too much if their enthusiastic reactions were any indication—she climbed into the back of the taxi. They pulled around the circle fronting the airport and onto a highway heading away from San José. Ella leaned forward.

"Diego said your name was Marvin. That's not a...a Tico name, is it?"

"Is *Norte Americano*." He glanced in the rearview mirror, his dark eyes bright with amusement. "*Mi madre* give me this name. It makes *las turistas* laugh when they hear it so they remember and hire me again."

She returned his smile. "And does it work? Do you get more business than the other cabbies?"

"Two times as much," Marvin boasted.

The highway narrowed as they continued toward the mountains. "How far is it to Milagro?" Ella questioned. "Will we be there soon?"

"Not far. Two, three *horas*. *Más o menos*."

"Three hours!"

"*Es problema*?" He looked in the mirror again and stomped harder on the accelerator. "For you, *Señora*, I drive *muy rapido*. Very fast. But most the roads, they are dirt and gravel. We go very fast, very slow so we miss all the holes. Okay?"

"No! That's not what I meant."

"It is not the roads that worry you?"

"No, not really." Although right at this moment, they did. But only because he spent more time looking in the mirror at her than at the road in front of them. "You can slow down. I don't mind."

"It is the money that worries you?" he guessed shrewdly, his foot easing a fraction from the accelerator. "The price of my taxi?"

Ella sighed. "I guess we should have settled on a fare before we left the airport."

"*No problema*," he claimed, in what she was fast realizing must be a stock reply. "You give me all your *colones* and I drive you to Milagro."

For one horrible, stomach-churning moment, all her worst nightmares about a woman alone in a foreign country sprang to life. Then Marvin began to chuckle.

"You're kidding, right?" she asked, the faintness of her voice a dead giveaway.

His grin widened. "*Sí*."

"Thank heavens."

"Is good joke, yes? Very funny."

She returned his smile. "Hysterical."

"I no charge you much. I have to go to Milagro anyway. We share a ride. Okay?"

"Thanks, I appreciate that."

"See those mountains?" He pointed in front of them toward a purple range of toothy crags. "We go there. I tell you all about them. You like that, yes?"

"I'd like that, thanks," she confirmed.

"Okay. The mountains, they are made of volcanoes. You know about our volcanoes? It makes good soil for *las fincas*. These are farms. You understand?"

She nodded, doing her best to listen attentively. But the stress of the last several weeks had taken its toll. Only a dozen more sentences registered before exhaustion overcame her and she fell sound asleep.

The screeching of brakes brought Ella violently awake. Marvin jerked the wheel to one side to avoid a pothole, sending her tumbling from one end of the seat to the other. Clipping the edge of a pit large enough to consume an entire fleet of trucks, they slewed precariously close to the edge of the gravel road. For a horrifying instant Ella stared out the window into a brilliant green abyss before Marvin brought the taxi back to the middle of the single lane. Struggling to right herself, she shoved the straw hat off her face and repositioned the sunglasses from the tip of her nose to the bridge.

"Ah, *Señora*. You are awake," he greeted her. "This is good."

"I—I must have been more tired than I'd realized." Insomnia had a way of doing that, she'd discovered over the past two months. "Have I been sleeping long?"

"Long time, but that is good. We get to Milagro very soon now."

"Oh, that's wonderful."

"See the coffee fields?" He waved his hand out the open window toward a blur of bright green they were passing at top speed.

She peered curiously at the tall bushlike trees, the first she'd ever seen. They climbed the hillside at an almost vertical slant. How anyone could possibly pick the bright red berries clustered among the shiny leaves, she couldn't begin to imagine.

"You are visiting someone in Milagro?" Marvin asked. "I know ever'body. I take you there."

"*No problema*, right?" she teased. "Actually, I'm here to see my husband."

Marvin swiveled to stare, his amazement almost comical. "You have a 'usband in Milagro?"

"His name is Rafe Beaumont. Do you know him?"

The words had no sooner left her mouth than Marvin slammed on the brakes and jerked hard on the wheel in an exact reenactment of his earlier maneuver. With a painful squeal, the taxi skidded to a halt at the side of the road. He jumped out of the car, his Spanish coming in such a torrent, she didn't have a hope of deciphering so much as a word.

"What is it? What's wrong?" she demanded.

He pointed at the coffee fields on the opposite side of the road, then said Rafe's name before launching into another irate deluge of Spanish. The way he practically spat out her husband's name suggested Marvin might be even more ticked off with Rafe than she was. With a final exclamation of fury, he circled the cab and threw open the trunk.

This could not be good.

Ella bolted from the backseat just in time to see him dumping her luggage on the side of the road. "Hey, wait a minute! You can't do that."

Marvin set his chin at a belligerent angle. "*Sí*, I can do that." He kept offloading her bags. "*Y tambien...sí*, I keep doing it."

She grabbed the nearest bag and tossed it back into the trunk, reloading as quickly as he unloaded. "What happened?" she panted. "What did I say?"

"*Lo siento*," he claimed, in what was clearly a lie. As far as she could tell, he didn't look the least bit sorry at all. "I can not take you to Milagro."

"Why? What's wrong?"

"Is your fault, okay?" He stopped unloading and faced her, planting his hands on his hips. "Your 'usband. You no tell me who he is."

"My fault!" She imitated his stance, fighting for breath in the higher elevation. "How was I to know it would make a difference? What does it matter if Rafe Beaumont is my husband? What did he do to you?"

"Not to me. *Mi sobrino*. My nephew. He fire Manuel."

"And because of that, you can't take me to Milagro?"

"*Sí*. It would be an insult to Manuel."

"How would it be an insult?" she questioned in exasperation. He didn't answer, simply went back to offloading her luggage. She hastened to switch tactics. "Look, you can't just strand me here on the side of the road. No one knows I'm coming."

Marvin's head emerged from the trunk to peer at her. "*Señor* Beaumont? Does he not know?"

"I wanted to surprise him." She pressed her advantage, small as it was. "What if no one else comes along to help me? Or what if the person who does come decides to rob me? Then it'll be your fault."

He hesitated. Clearly it went against the grain to leave a woman in such a precarious situation. "I can not take you. It is a matter of honor. *Comprende, Señora*?"

"No! I don't understand."

"You are his wife. His honor is your honor."

"Whatever Rafe has done has nothing to do with me, honor or no honor." She folded her arms across her chest. "And consider one more thing. If you think you had trouble with my husband before, it will be nothing compared to the trouble you have with him after this."

Marvin launched into another incomprehensible tirade. Finally he calmed enough to say, "I go to Milagro and send someone for you. It is best I can do. You wait here."

She glared at him, though with her sunglasses concealing her eyes, it lost most of its effectiveness. "Where would I go?"

"You wait here," he repeated. "Someone come very soon."

He climbed back into the cab and gunned the engine. Skidding away from the side of the road in a thick cloud of dust, he promptly dropped his rear wheel into a pothole. This one didn't appear quite large enough to swallow entire trucks, but it was sufficient to bring the cab to a grinding halt. Once again Marvin jumped from the vehicle, roundly cursing his fate and, if she didn't miss her guess, her, as well.

"It's your own fault," Ella told him. She pulled off her straw hat and used it to swipe at the dust clinging to her white sundress. To her dismay she only managed to transform the accumulated grime from ugly brown speckles to uglier brown streaks. Damn! "You shouldn't have left me behind. It's... it's divine retribution."

He scowled at the buried wheel, then at her. "You push, okay?"

She stared at him for a full minute. "You've got to be kidding."

His chin poked out again. "I do not kid with you. You push the car or I forget to send help from Milagro."

"I don't believe this." She tossed her hat in the direction of her luggage. "Buster, you just lost yourself a really good tip."

"Okay, but you push."

A big, fat raindrop plummeted from the sky, splattering in the dusty road midway between them. They both looked up at the same instant. Thick black clouds roiled above them, blotting out the brilliant blue sky. A chilly wind caught at her loose hair whipping the ebony strands across her throat and face. For an endless moment neither of them moved.

"Uh-oh," Marvin understated their predicament.

"That does it." Ella crossed to where her luggage had been dumped and seated herself on the largest of the suitcases. She removed the sunglasses she no longer needed and dropped them into her purse. Then she fixed Marvin with the steely gaze she'd learned so well from Rafe. "I'm not moving until you agree to take me to Milagro with you. If I'm going to get soaked, so are you."

He stared at her, his mouth dropping open. "*Madre de Dios*! *La Estrella*!"

She lifted an eyebrow. "Excuse me?"

"*La Estrella*! You are *La Estrella*."

"No, I'm Ella Beaumont."

"*Sí, sí. Señora* Beaumont." He bobbed his head up and down and beamed as though she were the answer to all his prayers. "*La Estrella. Lo siento, Estrella*. I did not know it was you."

She regarded him with deep suspicion. "Who is this *Estrella* person?"

"It is you. You are *la profecía*."

"The prophecy?"

"*Sí*. The prophecy." He slanted a nervous glance skyward. "Hurry, please. The rain come very hard. We must go."

Ella gnawed on her lower lip. She didn't have a clue what had just happened, but she'd be a fool not to take advantage of it. "Load my luggage first."

"And then you push, yes?"

"You won't leave me?"

He covered his heart with his hand. "My word of honor, *Estrella*."

By the time the luggage had been returned to the trunk, it had begun to rain in earnest. Within seconds, she was soaked through, her hair plastered to her neck and the side of her face. Great. Now she'd show up on Rafe's doorstep looking little better than the proverbial drowned rat.

Marvin climbed behind the wheel of the taxi and peered back at her. "Push, *Estrella*. Push!"

Flattening her palms against the filthy rear panel, she obediently shoved with all her strength. The wheel spun, kicking up a stream of mud and grit that covered her from head to toe. Just as her strength gave out, the cab bounced free. With the abrupt loss of support, Ella fell forward, plunging into the mud and water choked pothole. With a shriek of frustration, she scrambled out the other side, minus one sandal.

"Damn you, Rafe Beaumont," she muttered beneath her breath. She stood in the middle of the road, soaked to the skin and dirtier than she'd ever been before in her life. "If you don't fall in love with me after this, I swear I'll make you pay big time."

Marvin stuck his head out of the window. "You do good work, *Estrella*! Hurry. Get in before the road washes away."

Slogging with uneven steps through the rapidly deepening muck, she reached the taxi. "I'm really dirty, Marvin," she warned.

"My cab, it will clean. Get in. Get in."

She didn't waste her breath arguing further, but climbed in and collapsed against the backseat. Marvin thrust the car into gear and took off. Water runneled from her hair and dress forming a muddy pool around her half-shod feet and she wondered idly if Rafe would even recognize her. She fingered her wedding band. Grit filled the creases and she took the least dirty corner of her skirt and wiped it clean. Seconds later it gleamed a golden promise and she smiled in spite of herself.

"Not long until we get there, *Estrella*," Marvin reassured. He shot her an anxious glance in the rearview mirror. "If you don't let the road wash out, it would help."

"Excuse me?"

"The road, you keep it from washing down the mountain, okay?"

"And just how am I supposed to do that?"

"You are *La Estrella*," he said reasonably. "You must know how."

"Oh, really? Well, I have news for you. I haven't a clue." She peered outside and shivered. The rain was coming down so hard she couldn't see the coffee trees any longer. What she wouldn't give for a hot shower and some dry clothing—or even a spare sandal. "Tell me about this prophecy," she requested through chattering teeth. "How did I get involved? I've never even heard of Milagro until just recently."

Marvin fiddled with the controls for the heater and a blast of warm air issued from the vents. "The prophecy has been here a long time. It says that when the two golden *estrellas*—stars—appear in the midnight sky, happiness and *prosperidad* will return to Milagro."

"I don't understand... How does that make me this *Estrella*?"

"It is your eyes, *Señora*. They are the golden stars. And your hair. It is the color of a midnight sky."

"Uh-huh." She waited for the punch line. When it didn't come, she prompted, "Because I have dark hair and odd-colored eyes, you think I'm the one who fulfills this prophecy? You're kidding, right?"

"No, *Señora*. To the people of Milagro the prophecy is no joke. They have waited a long time for you. We have many problems that you must put right." He flashed her a quick, deferential look in the mirror. "First you must convince *Señor* Beaumont to hire Manuel once again."

She stared in alarm. "I'm not sure I can do that. *Señor* Beaumont is a very stubborn man."

"We have noticed that about him. But you will find a way, *Estrella*. The villagers, we depend on you."

She closed her eyes, too exhausted to figure a way to set him straight. She had enough problems with Rafe without taking on the town's troubles, as well. "How much longer?" she asked.

"Not far." Marvin whipped around a curve guided, she guessed, more by instinct or memory than by sight. Four hairpins later he said, "This is Milagro. We go just a little further to the top of the ridge."

She squinted out the window but didn't see a town, let alone a ridge. It wasn't until they'd reached a tall stucco wall and a set of iron-wrought gates that the rain eased enough for her to realize that they'd arrived at Rafe's home.

"*La Finca de Esperanza*," Marvin announced.

The gates stood open and he pulled through them. A long drive ended in a formal circle in front of a sprawling ranch house. The minute Marvin cut the engine, the rain stopped and the sun broke through the clouds.

"*Gracias, Estrella*. You kept the road from washing away and have brought the sun."

"Look. I had nothing to do with ending the rain or I'd have taken care of it a lot sooner than this." She glared at her ruined sundress. "A heck of a lot sooner."

She'd wasted her breath, she realized. Marvin had moved out of hearing range and was busily stacking her luggage on the tile entranceway. Ella stepped from the cab and gathered her energy for the next battle—the one she'd undoubtedly wage with her husband.

As though the thought alone had summoned him, Rafe appeared in the doorway. Without a word of acknowledgment, Marvin deposited the last of her suitcases and disappeared around the side of the house. Apparently, his odd view of honor kept him from hanging around.

Ella drew in a deep breath, wishing she looked a little better—at least a little cleaner. "Hello, Rafe."

CHAPTER SIX

RAFE stood for a long moment without speaking, a lit cigarette held negligently between his fingers. He lifted it to his mouth and inhaled, his gaze switching from Ella to the damp luggage at his feet. "You want to come in?" he asked with gentle irony, flicking the still-burning butt into the garden. "Or would you prefer I hose you down first?"

"That might be wise. Pushing cabs out of potholes during a downpour can be a bit . . . messy." She glanced in the direction he'd thrown the cigarette. A thin plume of smoke drifted up through the bright red hibiscus blossoms decorating a nearby bush. "Dad mentioned you'd taken up smoking. I told him he must be mistaken."

"You always did have too good an opinion of me, *amada*. I'll have to see what I can do to correct that." He stepped from the threshold and gestured toward the open doorway. "Welcome to my home. You can shower and change before we talk."

"Thanks, I'd appreciate that."

"After which I'll return you to the airport."

A dozen arguments leapt to her lips, but she suppressed every one of them. She had no intention of quarreling on the front doorstep. She'd save that for his study or library or wherever else he conducted private discussions.

It turned out to be an office.

"You look much better," Rafe commented when she joined him a full hour later.

"Thanks. I feel much better, too."

She'd taken her time preparing for this meeting, keenly aware that she'd only have this single opportunity to convince him she should stay. The outfit she'd chosen was one of her favorites—a short, fitted skirt in bridal ivory and a matching silk shell. To counterbalance the rather formal effect, she'd kept her hairstyle loose and simple by brushing it into a glossy cloud that framed her shoulders. She also kept her jewelry simple, limiting herself to a pair of gold earrings and her wedding band.

"I think that shower rated as a religious experience," she commented, glancing around the room. It was decisively masculine—trimmed in mahogany, starkly furnished and smelling of smoke. By conducting their interview here, Rafe had trapped her within the boundaries of his territory. It was a calculated maneuver, she realized, one designed to make it more difficult to turn the tables on him. Still she had no choice but to try. "I appreciate your hospitality."

"I'm pleased I could accommodate you." He gestured toward the chair in front of his desk. "Have a seat and tell me why you've come. I assume it's to discuss my plan in regards to your parents. If so, you're wasting your breath."

She did as he requested, glancing at him curiously. "Plan?"

"You're right," he conceded with a shrug. "To call it a plan is an inaccurate assessment of my intent. Perhaps 'threat' would be more concise."

Comprehension dawned. "You mean your threat to destroy my parents financially if they don't end the Cinderella Balls."

He cocked an eyebrow. "Have I made any other threats?"

Her mouth quivered on the verge of a smile. "No. I believe that's the only one—at least toward us. I can't speak for anyone else, however." She tilted her head to one side. "Have there been others?"

"Not that I can recall." Amusement lit the stormy depths of his eyes. "To the best of my knowledge, you and your parents have the honor of being the first."

"I'm relieved to hear it," she murmured dryly. "Of course, I'd be more relieved if we were also the last. Better yet, I'd prefer for you to give up the practice altogether."

"I'm sure you would. But enough of this, Ella," he said with a hint of impatience. "If you haven't come in an attempt to change my mind, or to offer me a written guarantee that the balls will end, then why have you come?" He reached for the half-empty pack of cigarettes littering his desk and shook one free.

"It's quite simple, Rafe." She fought the nervous dread knotting in the pit of her stomach. If she didn't miss her guess, her gallant host was about to become an infuriated husband. "I've come home."

His brows lowered ominously and he froze in the act of lighting his cigarette. "Pardon me? Did you say, home?"

"Yes, home." She stood and leaned across the desk, plucking the cigarette and match from between his fingers. "I always thought smoking a nervous habit. A crutch. But that can't be right. *You* aren't in need of a crutch, are you, Rafe?" Keeping her gaze fixed on him, she snapped the cigarette in two and blew out the match, tossing them both into a nearby ashtray.

Her perfume drifted toward him like the smoke from the match, filling his lungs with a seductive scent instead of an acrid one. With a muttered exclamation, he shoved back his chair, leaving his pack of cigarettes behind. "What the *hell* are you doing here, Ella? And I want the truth."

She took her time reseating herself. "It's quite simple."
She crossed her legs and smoothed the silk skirt along
her thighs, keenly aware that he watched her every
movement. "You married me. Now you're stuck with
me."

"You know why I married you," he informed her
through gritted teeth.

"Yes, I know. You want me. Well, guess what?" She
held his gaze, her feelings reflected in that one forthright
look. "I want you, too."

He reached for his cigarettes again, freezing at the betraying gesture. With a growl of annoyance, he grabbed
the pack and viciously crumpled it. "This isn't going to
work," he announced, tossing the crushed remains into
the trash. "I'll arrange a return flight for you first thing
in the morning."

She shook her head, her hair swirling in a graceful
arc around her shoulders. "I'm not going anywhere. Not
yet. Not until we've sorted this out."

His fist crashed against the teak tabletop. And that's
when she saw it. *He still wore his wedding band*. It caught
the rays of sunlight streaming in the window and sparkled
in a bright, golden promise.

"We sorted out our differences two months ago," he
rasped. "If you'll recall, our marriage ended as rapidly
as it began."

"That's where you're wrong. You see . . ." She steeled
herself to deliver her next little bombshell, somewhat
bolstered by the sign of commitment he carried on his
finger. "I have no intention of releasing you from your
vows until I'm convinced you have no feelings for me."

"Feelings? Our marriage has nothing to do with
feelings," he practically roared. "Our marriage is a
travesty, one of my own making, I admit. But at least
I had the good sense to walk away before it
went too far."

She leaned forward in the chair, her hands clutching the armrests in a white-knuckle grip. "Well, I refuse to walk away. I've loved you for almost six years and I'm not going to ruin my one chance for happiness because you're too pig-headed to take a chance. If you want to get rid of me, you'll have to physically throw me out."

He surged to his feet. "Do you think I won't?"

"You may try." She stood, as well. "But we both know what will happen the minute you put your hands on me. If you carry me anywhere, it won't be out the front door. It'll be to your bed to finish what we started two months ago."

"Don't tempt me to prove you wrong!"

"Let me make it easy for you." She opened her arms. "Go ahead, Rafe. I'm all yours. Pick me up and we'll see whether we end this on the front step or in your bedroom."

Fury exploded in his diamond-hard eyes, along with a blazing passion. He started around the desk toward her, his strides eating up the distance separating them. She knew a momentary twinge of fear, but it died as swiftly as it was born. He could fight and struggle and snarl all he wanted. It wouldn't do any good. What existed between them couldn't be denied any more than it could be controlled. A single kiss would shatter every purpose but one...

To finish what he'd started on their wedding night.

He slung a hand around her waist, hauling her against him. "You shouldn't have come back. I swear, you'll regret it."

"Don't you understand? That's a chance I had to take."

With a frustrated groan he seized her lips with an avid greed and gave back a wealth of passion. If he'd thought to employ restraint, it was rapidly lost beneath the ardent response his touch elicited. Her desire was as genuine as it was unchecked. Not once in all the time he'd known her had she tried to conceal her feelings for him. Never coy, never shy, never reluctant, she gave with unstinting generosity.

"Rafe, please."

Her urgent whisper scorched the air between them. He backed her toward his desk, ripping her blouse loose from her waistband. She didn't protest. He lifted her onto the edge, thrusting the short skirt to her waist and stepping between her legs. She held him tighter. With a harsh groan, he palmed the pale expanse of thigh between the top of her stockings and her lace-trimmed panties. Her silken lips beneath his mouth threatened to destroy him—her silken skin beneath his fingers nearly unmanned him.

She was everything he could ever want in a woman. If he could wrap himself in this moment, he would. But to take her on his desk with such callous disregard...

"Not here," he muttered with a groan.

"You know I won't refuse you." Her eyes burned with her need. "You're my husband."

"And you're my wife. At least in name."

"You could change that."

"Not here," he repeated. "And not now."

He closed his eyes and leaned into her softness, gathering the remanents of his control. Her breasts cushioned his face and he could feel her heart fluttering beneath his cheek. He took a deep breath and reluctantly pulled back. Holding out his hand, he helped her off the desk.

To Ella's dismay, her fingers were notably unsteady as she straightened her clothing. Not that she was the only one affected. From the corner of her eye she caught Rafe reaching for his cigarettes. It took a split second for him to remember what he'd done with them. When he did, he released a harsh sigh of frustration.

Tucking her blouse into her skirt, she gave him a direct look. "Well?" she asked with a determined show of mettle. "Did we settle that particular question?"

Furious color raced across his peaked cheekbones. "*Eres mío!*" he whispered roughly. "You are mine. And your fate is sealed. I give you one week. You understand? One week!"

Before she could decide whether that was good news or bad, a brief knock sounded on the door behind them before bursting open. Marvin and a small, lovely Tico woman stood there, their mouths agape.

"*Perdone, Señor,*" the woman said with a gasp. She started to leave, but then stole a second, closer look at Ella. "Marvin! *Tiene derecho! Es La Estrella. Está aquí! Por fin está aquí.*"

"Chelita, what's going on?" Rafe demanded. "What the hell are you talking about?"

She gestured toward Ella, a becoming flush tinting her cheeks. "The *Señora*. She is *La Estrella*. I did not believe Marvin, but he is right. She has come to fulfill the prophecy. She has finally come."

"The prophecy? You think Ella—" Rafe turned and glared at the cabdriver. "What are you up to, Marvin? What rumors are you spreading about my wife?"

"They are not rumors, but truth," Marvin protested. "Look at her, my friend. She is the prophecy, come as promised. Just because you are too blind to see what is right before your eyes, does not mean the rest of us are."

"She is not the fulfillment of some prophecy, she's Ella Mont—" He shut his eyes, cursing beneath his breath. "Ella Beaumont. My wife. *Not La Estrella.*"

But he was talking to thin air. Chelita and Marvin had vanished from the doorway, the sound of their excited, chattering voices growing ever more distant.

"I guess I should have mentioned . . ." Ella said hesitantly. "Marvin got it into his head that I'm the fulfillment of some prophecy and I haven't been able to convince him otherwise.''

"That's just great." He paced the room like a caged beast. "Marvin and my housekeeper are two of the biggest gossips in the area. By the end of the day it will be all over the village that I harbor *La Estrella* beneath my roof."

"Is that so bad? If it gives them hope—"

"Hope? What good will hope do them?" Rafe questioned caustically. "Will it fill their children's bellies with food? Will it get the coffee crop picked? Will it put *colones* in their hands? I don't think so."

"The coffee crop?" She frowned. "Marvin seemed terribly upset about something to do with the coffee fields. But he spoke in Spanish and I didn't understand."

Rafe sighed, his mouth set in grim lines. "The workers are on strike. Marvin's nephew, Manuel, has told them not to pick the beans."

No wonder Manuel had been fired. And how interesting that Marvin had neglected to mention that part. "Why are they striking?"

"Because I plan to sell *Esperanza*."

"Sell your plantation?" She stared in disbelief. "But, it's your home. It's been in your mother's family for generations. Why—"

"Enough, Ella." He cut her off brusquely. "This need not concern you."

"But it does concern me," she argued. "If I'm to live here—"

"Which you are not."

"A matter still open to discussion," she corrected. "If I'm to live here, then I'd like to help."

"You can't help. Don't you understand? This prophecy they speak of promises happiness and prosperity to the people of Milagro."

"I know. Marvin explained it to me."

"Then you must realize how impossible the situation is. How do you plan to fulfill this prophecy? They expect you to perform miracles." His tone turned sardonic. "Or did you just happen to pack a dozen or so in your suitcase?"

"Don't be ridiculous."

"Ridiculous? Be careful where you point fingers, *amada*. I'm not the one claiming to be *La Estrella*."

"I never claimed—"

"Nor have you managed to deny it." He rested a hip on the edge of his desk, the dark material of his trousers pulled taut across his muscled thighs. "What happens when you are unable to give them what they expect?"

"Is happiness and prosperity so difficult to achieve?" she asked gently. "If prosperity is dependent on picking coffee beans, than all we need to do is find a way to return the workers to the fields."

He lifted an eyebrow. "Oh, really. Is that all? How little you know."

"How can I know any more, if you won't tell me?" she flung back.

"I'm telling you now. There is no room for compromise with the villagers. They will not work. So much for their prosperity. And their happiness? What will you do to gain that, *princesa*?" He folded his arms across his chest. "Wave your magic wand and grant their dearest wish."

She shrugged. "It might be just that simple."

"Then you are as foolish as they."

"If you consider it foolish to believe in the possibility of happiness and miracles, then yes. I'm a fool."

"That's not what I meant."

"I suspect it's exactly what you meant. But I don't mind." She leaned against the door leading to the central corridor and regarded him intently. "Do you realize that it's New Year's Day?"

"Is it?" He thrust a hand through his hair. It was longer than when she'd last seen him, falling heavily across his forehead and along the nape of his neck. "As a matter of fact, I'd forgotten."

"Then I'm glad I'm here to remind you. Because today offers the chance for a new beginning."

"Meaning?"

"Meaning that as of today I start my campaign to restore your faith. I suspect you're too cynical to convince right away. But eventually, I hope to change that."

"It won't happen," he stated with cold assurance. "Not in a week. Not in a month. Not even if you had a full year."

"You're so certain?"

"I'm positive."

"Well, I don't agree." She thought fast. "I'll bet that before I leave I can perform a few miracles on you, too—like restoring your trust and your faith. And maybe, just maybe," she suggested daringly, "I can even restore your belief in love."

A bitter coldness swept his expression, his eyes turning a bleak, slate gray. "You will lose this bet, *amada*."

"But if I win—"

He nailed her with an unyielding gaze. "Let us be clear. If I could, I'd send you home right now. So much for faith and new starts. Unfortunately, to return you to Nevada is no longer possible. At least, not yet."

"Because of the prophecy?"

His mouth twisted. "I'd rather not be the one to drive *La Estrella* away. Better she be run off by the good people of Milagro once they realize she's a fraud. My guess is that will take about a week, which is fortunate since that's all the time you have."

"You're far too generous."

"More generous than you know."

"In that case, it looks like I have my work cut out for me. Which reminds me..." She shifted from her stance at the door and approached him with a concerned frown. "Perhaps you can help me perform my first miracle. I'm supposed to convince you to rehire Manuel."

He laughed, the sound deep and sincere and incredibly appealing. "For that, *amada*, you will need a true miracle. I have vowed that Manuel won't be rehired unless the workers return to the coffee fields. They won't return unless I promise not to sell the plantation. And that I will never do. In fact, I meet with the buyers in the morning to finalize the terms of our agreement."

"You never did say why you want to sell." A sudden thought struck and alarm darkened her eyes. "Rafe... You're not in financial trouble, yourself? You don't *have* to sell, do you?"

"Yes, I have to sell. But not for financial reasons."

"Then—"

"It's personal. And as I've said before, none of your concern." He walked past her and stood by the door. "Come. I'll make sure the rest of your luggage has reached your room. Would you like Chelita to help you unpack?"

"I can manage to transfer my clothing from suitcase to dresser drawer without assistance, thanks." She joined him at the door. "Despite what you think I'm quite self-sufficient."

"I'm relieved to hear it." He stared down at her. "And just so you know. You may claim to love me, but they're just words. There can only be one explanation for your presence. And that's to prevent me from harming your parents. Any other excuse is a smoke screen."

"That's not true. Besides, if you can actually do as you claim—affect their finances, as you say—that means you could have done it at any point over the past five years. But you didn't." She smiled up at him. "If you'd really wanted revenge, you'd have taken it long before this."

"Is that what you think?"

"It's what I believe."

"You consider me incapable of harming your parents?" he questioned curiously.

"Of course. I—"

He cupped the side of her face, sealing her lips with his thumb. "Listen to me now. And listen carefully. I will not be diverted from my purpose by you or anyone else. To think otherwise is to risk more disillusionment. Will your parents give me my agreement?" He caressed the length of her mouth before releasing her.

She moistened her lips. "I haven't asked them to, no."

"Then fair warning. Their fate is in your hands."

"No, Rafe," she countered. "It's in yours."

He didn't respond. Instead, he opened the door and stepped to one side, bringing the interview to an end. She'd both lost ground and gained ground, she realized as she returned to her bedroom. She'd won the right to remain at Rafe's *finca*—for the moment. But only at the risk of her parents' financial security. If she were smart, she'd give him what he'd demanded and leave. Unfortunately, to do that meant relinquishing any chance of a future with him. She didn't doubt that her marriage would last only as long as she continued to have something he wanted.

A light tapping at the door interrupted her thoughts. "Ella?" Shayne peeked into the bedroom, tucking a strand of honey-blond hair into the formal twist at the nape of her neck. She gazed at Ella, her huge, dark eyes oddly expressionless. "May I come in?"

"Shayne!" Ella ran to greet her, enveloping the younger girl in a warm embrace. It was returned with a surprising fierceness before Shayne pulled sharply away. "It's been so long."

"Five years. Five very long years." Aside from a nervous knotting of her fingers, Shayne's composure appeared picture-perfect. "It's lovely to see you again."

Tears pricked Ella's eyes. "And just look at you..." She scanned her one-time friend for changes—astonished by how many there were. "You're taller, I think, and—" Cooler. More remote. More like Rafe. "Why, you're all grown up," she finished lamely.

"It was bound to happen sooner or later." Shayne took a hesitant step into the room. "I stopped by to...to apologize. This entire situation with Rafe is my fault."

"Your fault?" Ella moved away from the door. "Come in and talk to me while I unpack. Why do you think any of this is your fault?"

Shayne perched on the edge of the bed, her posture stiffly erect, her attitude far too reserved for someone who'd just turned twenty-three. "The ticket Rafe used to attend the ball was mine."

"Yours!"

"He had a fit when he found out what I'd planned, as I'm sure you can imagine."

Ella shook her head in confusion. "I don't understand. How did you manage to get a ticket? Guests have to fill out an application well in advance. We have everyone screened by a security company. I'd have known if you had applied."

"Oh, I circumvented that," Shayne revealed. "I talked a friend into applying for me. I planned to use his ticket once he received it, but I'd forgotten that you use special messengers to deliver them. It was a foolish error."

"The application was in his name?"

"Yes." A strand of hair came loose again and with an impatient grimace, she tucked it behind her ear. "When the messenger arrived to deliver the ticket, it caused quite a commotion in the village. Eventually word reached Rafe. He realized at once what I'd done."

"I see..." Ella gazed at Shayne in concern. "Why in the world—"

"I'm sure you can guess. I thought Chaz might be there." Her response was stark. To the point. And utterly devastating. "It's the same reason I tried to attend the Anniversary Ball. If it hadn't been for the accident..." She trailed off and shrugged.

Ella inhaled sharply. "That's when you were hurt? On the way to the Anniversary Ball?"

Shayne glanced at Ella uncertainly. "Didn't you know about that?"

"Not until recently." She crossed to sit on the bed, catching Shayne's hands in her own. "Sweetheart, I wish you'd called instead of going to so much trouble. I could have told you Chaz wouldn't be there."

A hint of dark emotion flitted across the younger girl's face before vanishing beneath a mask of composure. "You're certain?"

"I checked the list myself."

Shayne bowed her head. "It was stupid, I know. If I'd just left well enough alone, Rafe wouldn't have bothered to go after you again. That's why he's so determined to end the Cinderella Balls. Because of me."

"You let me worry about that. He might still surprise you."

"For your sake, I hope so." Shayne hesitated before rushing into speech. "There's something else I've been meaning to ask." Again came that flash of emotion and again she brought it under swift control. "You never told Rafe what happened, did you?"

"At the Cinderella Ball five years ago?" Ella clarified. "No, I didn't."

"Why didn't you just tell him I'd lied? That you hadn't invited me?"

"For one simple reason. I'd never do anything to harm your relationship with Rafe."

"I—" She bit her lip. "Thank you."

"Don't thank me." Ella's gaze held a flash of fire. "I didn't do it for your sake, Shayne. I did it for his."

"I see." She seemed to gather herself. "I owe you an apology. A long overdue apology. I took advantage of you. Worse, I ruined your relationship with my brother. I realize nothing I can say now will ever make up for the wrong I did. But I am sorry."

"You were only seventeen. I understood."

"That's more than Rafe would have," Shayne said candidly. "Still, I hurt you both. Terribly. I hope you can forgive me one day."

Ella smiled. "I forgave you long ago." She tilted her head to one side. "You've never told him the truth, either. Have you?"

"I've tried," Shayne replied. "I've gotten as far as admitting it was my fault. But he won't listen. I'm not sure he wants to hear the truth."

"And what truth is that?"

For a brief instant, her composure shattered and Ella caught a glimpse of a grief-torn woman. "I still love Chaz McIntyre. It's been five years and nothing's changed."

"Is that why you keep coming back? You hope to find him again?"

Shayne nodded. "Rafe had the marriage annulled because I was underage. You want to know the funny part?" A heartbreaking smile chased across her mouth. "If the ball had been just one day later, I'd have been eighteen. And the ending to my story might have been very different."

"Shayne—"

She stood abruptly, pulling her hands free. "I can't talk about it anymore. Excuse me, won't you?" She paused at the door, her back rigid, her hand clinging to the knob. "Dinner's at seven. I'll see you then."

The door shut softly behind her.

Ella closed her eyes. There had to be something she could do. Some way she could help to put Shayne's life right again.

It would seem that *La Estrella* had yet another miracle to perform.

CHAPTER SEVEN

"I'M SO pleased you've come, Ella," Shayne attempted to break the silence at dinner that evening. "Is this a...prolonged visit?"

"Yes. Very prolonged."

"No," Rafe retorted at the same instant. "It will be very brief."

Chelita paused in the act of pouring him a glass of wine, her expression patently horrified. "Oh, *Señor* Beaumont, you will not make *La Estrella* leave! The villagers, we need her."

"*La Estrella*?" Shayne questioned, glancing from one to the other. "What's she talking about?"

Rafe released his breath in an impatient sigh. "I have no intention of making her do any such—Chelita, the wine?"

The housekeeper hastened to right the bottle before it overflowed the glass. "Oh! *Lo siento, Señor* Beaumont. It's just that we are so happy. She has finally come after all this time and—"

"No one told me she'd finally come," Shayne complained. "Where is she? Who is she? Would someone please tell me what's going on?"

"Um. I'm what's going on," Ella confessed. "I guess I forgot to mention it earlier. It seems that Marvin and Chelita have gotten it into their heads that I'm *La Estrella*."

Shayne's mouth dropped open *"You're—"*

"Chelita," Rafe interrupted with a frown. "Unless I'm very much mistaken, this wine tastes suspiciously like champagne."

"*Sí, Señor*. I knew you would want to celebrate the arrival of *La Estrella*."

"You knew this, did you?"

"It is obvious," she said, missing his sarcasm. "Everyone is so excited. Now will come the happiness and prosperity her arrival promises. We should celebrate such a miracle."

"Unless, of course," Shayne said in an innocent-sounding voice, "my dear brother sends her home."

"Damn it, Shayne!"

"Send her home?" Chelita slammed the bottle onto the table, suspicion swiftly replacing her earlier enthusiasm. She glared at Rafe. "You will take *La Estrella* from us, *Señor* Beaumont? You would do that to the people of Milagro?"

A muscle leapt in his jaw. "I have no intention of sending her anywhere."

"Then I'm permitted to stay?" Ella inserted smoothly. "For longer than a week?"

All eyes pivoted to Rafe.

He drained his glass in a single swallow and set the flute on the table with enough force to make the fragile crystal vibrate in protest. "I am not accustomed to being interrogated in my own home."

"But, *La Estrella*—" Chelita began in protest.

"*La Estrella* is free to come and go as she pleases." His gaze switched to Ella, a silent order glittering in the wrathful gray depths of his eyes. "Before long, I expect it will please her to return home. End of discussion. Chelita, serve the dinner, *por favor*."

The housekeeper folded her arms across her chest. "Not until you promise to keep her."

"Chelita!"

"Fine! I will serve the dinner. And I will bring a wine more to your liking." Snatching up the bottle, she headed for the kitchen, continuing to voice her complaints in rapid Spanish.

"Gee, I sort of liked the champagne," Shayne murmured. "I thought it a nice touch."

"I believe you've caused enough trouble for one evening," Rafe said, frowning at his sister. Then his eyes softened. "But it is good to see you so animated. Perhaps Ella's visit has had some benefit, after all."

"Three cheers for me," Ella muttered.

Her comment drew his attention. "May I suggest you change the subject to something less volatile, *amada*? Or would you care to return to my office and continue our previous discussion? We could pick it up where we last left off."

Choosing the safer of the proffered choices, Ella addressed her sister-in-law. "How's your mosaic work going? I look forward to seeing your latest pieces."

It was unquestionably the wrong topic to choose. The color bleached from Shayne's cheeks and she copied Rafe's example, swallowing her champagne in a single gulp before returning the flute to the table. Once again the fragile crystal sang in protest. "I haven't done any mosaic work since... In a long time. I'm studying to be an accountant now."

"An accountant!" Ella couldn't conceal her distress. "But you're so talented. How could you—"

"Dinner, it is ready," Chelita interrupted, pushing a wooden serving cart into the dining room. After replacing the wine, she removed a silver cover from the first dish and set a steaming plate in front of Ella. "For you, *Estrella*, I have made a special Tico meal called *casado*."

Shayne began to laugh. "That's meant to be amusing, Ella. A Tico joke. You see *casado* in Spanish means a married man. The dish is supposed to be what a husband can routinely expect from his wife once he's safely caught and wed. It's sort of a pot luck—a little of everything. There's rice and beans—"

"*Y picadillos*," Chelita added.

"That's a mixture of potatoes, string beans, meat, tomatoes...oh, heavens. Just about everything minced and thrown together with some spices. Let me see, what else has she given you? Spaghetti, salad, eggs and— Is that *corvina*, Chelita?"

"*Sí, corvina.*"

"And sea bass."

Ella smiled her appreciation. "It looks wonderful."

"It tastes wonderful, too," Shayne assured her. "Chelita is a marvelous cook."

The housekeeper served Shayne next and finally Rafe. Crossing to her cart, she began to swiftly roll it toward the kitchen.

"Chelita. One moment, if you please," Rafe said mildly.

Ella glanced up in alarm. She knew that tone of voice. It didn't bode well for any of them. Apparently, Chelita knew it, as well.

"I must get to the kitchen—" she began.

"First you will explain this." Exerting some effort, he managed to spear a cut of meat on the end of his fork. "Would you mind telling me what this...this black item is, please?"

"Steak," Chelita whispered, her gaze glued to the floor.

"Steak," he repeated, lifting it off the plate for a closer examination. "How interesting. And have you discovered a new method of cooking it, perhaps?"

She cleared her throat. "Why, yes, *Señor*. It is a new method."

"I see. And this new method . . . Is it one that involves leaving the meat on the grill until it shrivels up into an inedible lump of coal?"

"I think that's how it is prepared." She peeked at him from beneath her lashes. *"Gusta usted?"*

"No, Chelita. I don't like. If this is your clever way of preventing *La Estrella*'s eventual departure, it has failed." He returned the steak to the plate. "Be so kind as to take this to the kitchen and bring me a fresh meal."

"Sí, Señor," she replied in a subdued voice.

"And, Chelita?" He waited until he had her full attention. "No more experiments of this nature. I have told you *La Estrella* is welcome to stay as long as she wishes. Burning my dinner will not succeed in keeping her here any longer than she chooses to remain. Just as it didn't succeed in convincing me to rehire Manuel. Understand?"

With a quick nod, she fled.

The minute the housekeeper cleared the room, he turned on Ella. "This is your fault," he informed her.

"My fault? How could it possibly be my fault?"

"She wouldn't dare risk her job in such a manner if she didn't believe prosperity and happiness awaited just around the corner. She undoubtedly expects *La Estrella* to remedy everything that goes wrong in her life. Including the loss of her employment."

"Well, I wouldn't let you fire her, that's for sure."

"Really?" He leaned back in his chair and fixed her with a curious gaze. "And just how would you go about stopping me?"

"I would hire her myself."

"A novel idea with only one unfortunate flaw."

"Which is?"

"You forget, *amada*. This is my home. Who works within its walls is up to me."

"And your wife has nothing to say about it?"

"No," he stated succinctly. "She doesn't. That being the case, may I recommend you do nothing to encourage Chelita or any of the others in their misguided beliefs. You are not this prophecy come to life. Nor can you fix their various problems. To attempt such a thing will only further complicate matters."

After a few moments of awkward silence, Shayne offered a new topic for them to pursue. Ella seized it with relief. She sympathized with Rafe's position in regard to the villagers and his dismay at their eagerness to believe in the prophecy. She just didn't agree. But until she could change his mind, the less said, the better. Once they'd finished eating, Chelita served *tacita de café*—a small cup of coffee—which Ella discovered typically concluded the meal.

"It's the estate's own blend and absolutely wonderful because it's processed with more care than larger commercial operations," Shayne said. "Our coffee is classified as an 'arabica strictly hard bean' which makes it one of the finest products in the world."

"I've always wondered how coffee was produced," Ella commented. "I saw the trees on my way here, but I didn't see any beans, just berries."

"The beans are hidden inside, two to a 'cherry,' except for the occasional peaberry which contains only one," Rafe explained. "When they turn red, they're ready to pick."

"I assume you don't wake up one morning to discover a field full of ripe cherries?" she teased.

He smiled. "No. It's an arduous job, requiring several return visits to the same tree. Once the coffee beans are picked, our particular variety is washed through several machines to remove the pulp. The beans are then left to ferment for a day for a variety of reasons, one of which is to add sharpness or acidity to the flavor. It makes a superior cup of coffee, don't you agree?"

"It's delicious," Ella said truthfully.

"I'm pleased you like it." He stood and to her utter astonishment leaned down and snatched a quick kiss. "I apologize for deserting you, but I have a phone call to make."

"That's all right," she said faintly. "I understand."

After he'd left, Shayne grinned. "So, how did you like your first lesson on coffee production?"

"It was fascinating." Ella poured herself another half cup and added a large dollop of warmed milk from the earthenware pitcher Chelita had provided. "In fact, I'd enjoy learning more."

Shayne made a face. "That's what you think. You're lucky Rafe decided to give you the shortened version or you might have found it far less fascinating. It's more complicated than he's making out."

"I can imagine."

"Listen, I have an idea." Shayne shifted her empty cup to one side and stood. "Why don't I take you to see the mosaic in the courtyard? Brother-dear would probably discourage my showing it to you if I suggested it. But since it's of you . . ."

"Of me?"

Shayne laughed at Ella's expression. "I'm kidding, or perhaps only half kidding. Actually, it's supposed to represent *La Estrella*. Would you like to see a rendering of your namesake?"

"I'd love to." Ella followed eagerly as Shayne led the way through the corridors toward the center of the ranch house. "Is it one of your designs?"

A momentary darkness slipped across Shayne's features. "No, though I did work on restoring it at one point."

"Shayne, what happened?" Ella asked gently as they stepped out into the central courtyard. Deep purple bougainvillea arched overhead and ferns leaned across the

pathway. Flaming heliconia and bright pink torch ginger
turned the area into a blaze of color. "Why did you give
up something that meant so much to you?"

A coolness settled into Shayne's dark eyes. "Creating
mosaics is a pipe dream, not a profession. Studying to
be an accountant is much more practical."

"That's your brother speaking."

"Yes, I suppose it is."

"What happened to the girl I knew?" Ella questioned
sadly. "Where has she gone?"

Shayne pushed ahead, her pace increasing. "She
doesn't exist anymore. She grew up."

"Growing up doesn't mean letting go of dreams."

Shayne laughed, the cynical sound particularly harsh
in the serene beauty of their surroundings. "That's
exactly what it means. You'll discover that for yourself
if Rafe has anything to say about it."

"I hope you're wrong."

"I'm not." Shayne gestured toward an open area
skirting a large fountain. "This is it. I'd stay, but I have
some computer work to finish before morning. Excuse
me, won't you?"

She'd blundered, Ella realized. She shouldn't have
pushed so hard. At least, not this soon. "Shayne, wait.
Please, don't go—" But she was ignored.

She didn't attempt a pursuit. There'd be time enough
to make amends at a later date. With a sigh of regret,
she turned her attention to the mosaic beneath her feet.
It was a fascinating piece. A brilliant rainbow of colors
coiled around the fountain seemingly at random, bright
at one end and fading to black at the other. At length,
she began to discern a pattern. And what she saw took
her breath away.

The bright swirl of colors was a woman's gown and
had been designed to wrap around the fountain as though
she knelt in prayer. The black section was her hair, the

mosaic tiles dusted with specks of silver so it did indeed look like a midnight sky. And the two golden stars... They were the woman's eyes—an oddly familiar shade between gold and amber.

When the two golden stars appear in the midnight sky, happiness and prosperity will return to Milagro.

Ella hadn't understood why Marvin thought the prophecy referred to a person instead of a celestial event. But now she did. If Marvin had seen this, it was no wonder he'd mistaken her for *La Estrella*. Whether it was Shayne's restoration work or the interpretation of the original artisan, the woman depicted in the tiles bore an uncanny resemblance to the face Ella saw in the mirror each morning.

A small sound captured her attention and she turned to peer toward the denser shadows in the far corner. Rafe stepped into the dusky light, a brandy snifter in hand. He gestured toward the mosaic. "The two of you have a lot of work to accomplish."

"So it would seem." She glanced at him uncertainly. "I thought you had a call to make. Have you been standing there long?"

"Long enough. My call was brief so I came out here to enjoy the sunset. If I hadn't so rashly disposed of my cigarettes, you'd have detected me the instant you and my sister arrived."

"That's... unfortunate."

"Because I overheard Shayne's comments?" He took a healthy swallow of brandy. "She said nothing I didn't already know."

"Rafe, there must be some solution to all these problems. You can't honestly believe that Shayne is better off as an accountant than doing the work she loves?"

"It doesn't matter what I think." He shoved his hand into his trouser pocket, and though he shrugged almost negligently, she noticed his fingers bunched into a fist.

"After the accident, she lost the heart to design. That's what your Cinderella Ball did to her."

"Isn't there anything—"

"Enough, Ella! You are not *La Estrella*. You cannot solve all the problems that exist here. To try risks more than just disappointment."

"Why do you say that?"

"Being the fulfillment of a prophecy is a dangerous business."

"Only to those who don't believe."

"*Dios!* Don't tell me you are buying the illusion, as well?" he demanded. "You're not here to bring happiness and prosperity to Milagro. Nor are you here to restore my faith or Shayne's. To try such a thing is to risk doing more harm than good."

"How can it hurt anyone to give them hope?"

"Because they believe in you. They trust you. Which means they can be led astray by you."

"Led?"

"You must realize... Where *La Estrella* leads, the villagers will follow."

She lowered her gaze to the mosaic, digesting his words. They offered some intriguing possibilities.

As though sensing the path her thoughts took, he warned, "Don't be diverted from your purpose, Ella, or you'll regret it. You've come to *Esperanza* for one simple reason—to try and reach a compromise in regards to your parents' situation. Stick to that and you have a chance of achieving some limited success."

"That's not why I'm here," came her instant denial. "I came because I—"

"Don't say it." The words were torn from him. "Not again."

"Is it so difficult to hear?" she asked regretfully.

"You confuse lust with love. Don't tempt me to show you the difference."

She glanced at him from beneath her lashes. "I wish you would."

He lifted the brandy snifter to his mouth and tilted it, draining the contents. Then he set it on the rim of the fountain and approached, grim purpose in every line of his body. She didn't wait. Taking the initiative, she slipped into his arms and caught his face between her hands.

The gathering of night was kind to him, gentling stark lines and softening taut planes. But the need torching his eyes rejected even that slight kindness. His gaze burned with the harsh light of necessity. Determined to give him what he craved, she tugged his head toward hers and kissed him.

He tasted of warmth and brandy and heady passion. Tilting her head to one side, she deepened the kiss, parting her lips and surging into the sweet tangy warmth. His groan slipped from his mouth to hers, full of primitive demand. It touched a primal chord she'd never known existed, resonating with a power that left her with no option but one.

To give herself body and soul to this man.

In the brief space from one breath to the next, he took control. His mouth consumed hers. It wasn't a gentle loving, but a hot, urgent mating. Taking. Plundering. Invading. His hands settled on her hips, cupping the narrow bones. With each frenzied kiss, his hold grew more aggressive. He surged against her, rocking rhythmically, fighting to get closer than cotton and silk would allow.

Her reaction was as instantaneous as it was violent. She shuddered in his arms, a desperate moan catching in the back of her throat. "Oh, please, Rafe," she whispered. "If this is lust, I'll take it."

He reared back as though she'd struck him. Thrusting her away, he snatched the brandy snifter from the rim

of the fountain. For a split second she thought he meant
to hurl it against the side of the house. Instead it shattered explosively within his grasp. For a long, shocked
moment, he stared at his hand. A trickle of blood spread
across the palm and he pulled the air into his lungs as
though it were a great effort.

"Rafe!" She started toward him, but he shook his
head, warning her off.

"You should not have come to *Esperanza*," he rasped.
He looked her full in the eyes. Where once passion had
blazed like a thousand candles, a terrible darkness had
descended, snuffing the light.

"How can you say that?"

"It is so simple, a child could see. You have no one
to protect you from harm as long as you remain here."
His mouth twisted. "No one to protect you from your
husband."

She held out a hand. "I don't need protection. I just
need you."

"No! Don't you understand? I will use you. I will
hurt you." He drew in on himself, raising an impenetrable wall between them. "I cannot allow that to
happen."

"For the love of heaven, Rafe. Explain it to me. You
can't allow what to happen?"

"I have destroyed a life once before by failing in my
duty, by failing to protect one of my own. I won't destroy another. And that's what would occur if this went
any further. I'd destroy you."

"You wouldn't. You couldn't."

"I will, *amada*, because it is in my nature to do so.
And nothing you can say or do will change that." He
inclined his head in an oddly formal manner. "Excuse
me while I see to my hand." And with that he turned
and disappeared into the night.

Ella didn't move for a long time. He'd destroyed a life once before by failing to protect one of his own? That could only refer to Shayne and the Cinderella Ball. She shook her head in confusion. She still didn't understand. Something more motivated his anger, his fierce drive to protect those he cared for. And until she found out what, their marriage didn't stand a chance.

Releasing a sigh of frustration, she took a final look at the mosaic. "Well, *Estrella*. It looks like Rafe was right. We do have a lot of work to accomplish. But thanks to him, I believe I've figured out how to perform our first miracle."

Bright and early the next morning Ella trekked down the dirt road to the village of Milagro. It was a beautiful day, the air dry, but far softer than the aridness she'd grown accustomed to in the desert. The amount of green also astounded her. If she didn't have a job to accomplish, she'd have stopped every few feet to examine a new tree or bush or flower. She grinned. Or ant trail. The first person she ran into when she reached Milagro was Marvin.

"*Estrella*," he greeted, clearly surprised by her presence. "You have come to visit us?"

"Actually, I've come for some help."

"But, of course. How may we assist you?"

"I'd like to pick coffee beans and I don't know how to do it. I'd hoped someone from the village could explain the process and loan me whatever equipment I might need."

His mouth fell open and he stared in astonishment. "You play a joke on Marvin, yes?"

"No. I'm quite serious." She glanced over his shoulder at the people who'd begun to gather in the street and offered her warmest and most confident smile. "Hello."

The response was typically Tico-friendly. Returned smiles and an occasional *"pura vida"* came from the ever-expanding crowd. Marvin turned and relayed her request in rapid Spanish. After several minutes of debate, he switched his attention back to her.

"You understand, we are on strike," Marvin began uncomfortably.

"Oh, I understand. I don't expect anyone to help me. But it's past time to pick, isn't it? And somebody has to do it." She shrugged. "I guess I'm that somebody."

Another man stepped forward. "It is my fault, *Estrella*. I am the one responsible for this strike."

"You must be Manuel." She looked at him, secretly surprised. She'd expected an angry activist. Instead she found a sincere young man with a bright smile and lively, intelligent eyes. She held out her hand. "I'm Ella Beaumont."

He took her hand in his. "It is a pleasure to meet you."

"Perhaps you could help?" she suggested. "If you would equip me with the supplies I need and then explain whatever I should know in order to pick the beans, it'll give us a chance to become better acquainted."

"I'd like that," Manuel instantly agreed. Intense curiosity crept into his nut-brown eyes. "You'll need a *canasta*. A wicker basket. And to protect your clothing, an apron would be wise."

Both were almost instantaneously produced, along with a straw shade hat. Ella accepted each with a pleasant smile and sincere thanks. Once outfitted, she started back up the hill with Manuel at her side.

"Why do you wish to pick the beans?" he asked. "Is it your hope to bring an end to the strike?"

"Yes," she admitted readily. "From what I gather, both you and my husband are stubborn men, each too proud to back down once you've taken a stance."

"That is an accurate assessment," he confessed with a charming smile. "However, there are reasons why we are forced to take opposing positions."

"Both are valid reasons, I'm sure," she said, trusting he'd catch her underlying meaning. Although she sympathized with the villagers, she wanted to be clear that she supported her husband above all else. "I'm hoping that if the villagers see *La Estrella* picking beans, they'll decide to help."

He glanced over his shoulder. "I expect you're right."

A quick look confirmed that they were being followed by a large crowd. "Once they're back at work, I'll try and convince Rafe to rehire you."

He lifted an eyebrow. "And how do you plan to do that?"

"Oh, I have an idea or two that might do the trick."

"I applaud your incentive. However, you must realize that I cannot follow my friends and family into the fields. *Señor* Beaumont would not stop the others from working. But he cannot allow me to do so until our differences are resolved. I must respect that, *Estrella*."

With each moment that passed, he impressed her more and more. She sent him a hesitant look. "You do know that I'm really not this *La Estrella*."

"Who is to say?" he replied with a shrug. He paused beneath the shade of a banana tree on the edge of the fields. "The people believe, which is the most important consideration. Your actions, as well as any inaction, will have a tremendous impact on them."

"Rafe said something similar," she admitted. "But surely it's better to do something than nothing."

Again he shrugged. "Time will tell."

"Your English is excellent, Manuel," she probed delicately. "What do you do aside from pick coffee beans— when you're not on strike, that is?"

He chuckled. "I am a botany student at the University of San José."

A sudden thought occurred to her. "And do you also provide love-struck young women with tickets to Cinderella Balls?"

"Guilty, I fear. Shayne wished to find her husband and I could not refuse her request." A faint flush tinted his angled cheekbones. "Especially when Chelita added her pleas to those of your sister-in-law's."

"I see," Ella said, struggling to keep a straight face. She slapped the wide-brimmed hat onto her head. "I guess I'm ready. What do I do?"

Amusement flashed in his eyes. "It's quite simple, *Estrella*. You pick anything that's red. Put it in your basket. And watch out for snakes." With a friendly smile and a cheerful *"buena suerte,"* he turned and trotted back toward the village.

"Manuel, wait a minute!" she called after him in alarm. "Snakes? What snakes?"

CHAPTER EIGHT

"*SEÑOR* Beaumont?" Chelita knocked on the door before stepping into his office.

"Yes?" He glanced up from his papers. "What is it?"

"*Los hombres malos son aquí.*"

He sighed, capping his pen and dropping it onto the blotter. "Just because they're interested in purchasing *Esperanza* doesn't make them bad."

"You are right. It makes them very bad," she retorted. "We will all lose our jobs when they take over *la finca*. Then the villagers will have to leave their mountain homes or they will starve. We will end up begging on the streets of San José." She shot him an ominous look. "Or worse."

He struggled to contain his annoyance. "I've told you a hundred times, the new owners won't do any such thing. Life will continue just as it always has."

"Of course, *Señor*. I am sure you are right. You want I should let them in?"

His brows lowered. "You've left my guests standing outside?"

"I did something wrong?" she asked innocently. A little too innocently.

This was getting out of hand. Never had he dealt with such blatant defiance. Never, that was, until his darling wife had arrived on his doorstep. "You know damned well you did something wrong!" He fought to lower his voice, a task becoming increasingly difficult with every hour his wife remained his wife. "Please admit the visitors and then ask Ella to join us."

"Er... who?" she asked in feigned bewilderment, her grasp of English miraculously vanishing.

"*La Estrella*. Remember her? The bearer of happiness and prosperity? Where is she? I'd like to introduce her."

Chelita blanched. "I'm not sure that is such a good idea."

His suspicion grew. "*Mi esposa*," he rasped. "*Dónde está?*"

"I, ah... I have forgotten your guests. I go let them in." She ducked out of the room.

"Chelita!"

She peeked nervously around the corner of the door. "*Sí, Señor?*"

"*Where...is...she?*"

"In the coffee fields," Chelita whispered, wringing her hands.

"The coffee fields." He fumbled for his pack of cigarettes with his bandaged hand, remembering an instant too late that he'd thrown them away. How could he have been so foolish? Of course, he knew how. One glance from a pair of pleading golden eyes and his common sense drained straight into his trousers. *Dios*! It was enough to drive a man to drink. "Chelita, would you be so good as to tell me what the *hell* my wife is doing in the fields?"

Her voice grew even softer. "Picking coffee beans."

Rafe's hand closed into a fist as he fought for control. It was a long time coming. Finally, he shoved back his chair and stood. Chelita edged toward the door, her eyes wide with apprehension.

"*Señor?* What do you intend to do?"

"I intend to go fetch my wife. You are to invite my guests in and serve them a cup of coffee while they wait. Is that clear?"

"*Café. Sí, Señor.* I will use the estate blend. And I will be polite. Very polite."

"What a novel idea."

He left the room and took the back way to the coffee fields. To his utter astonishment, the workers were all there, laughing and joking...and picking beans. He was keenly aware of the sudden silence and surreptitious glances he received as he strode along the row of bushy trees. It took him several minutes to discover which wide-brimmed hat concealed his wife.

"Oh, hello, Rafe. Isn't it a beautiful morning?"

She greeted him with remarkable nonchalance for a woman about to be strangled.

"I would like to speak with you, please."

"Sure. Go right ahead."

"Someplace more private, if you'd be so kind."

"Okay. But I should warn you—"

"You may warn me when we're alone."

He stripped off the basket harnessed around her waist, seized her arm and escorted her through the crowd of avidly watching villagers. As she passed, they quietly removed their baskets and sat down.

"I tried to warn you," she began breathlessly. "If I don't work, neither will they."

"That does not concern me at the moment. What does concern me is that my wife is picking coffee beans like a—"

"Like a common peasant?" she inserted blandly.

He clamped his jaw closed, waiting until he had sufficient mastery of his anger before continuing. "It is not appropriate for you to be here. The villagers know this, which is why they chose to go into the fields rather than continue with their strike. They cannot in good conscience allow you to work unaided."

She smiled at him from beneath the shade of her straw hat. "I assumed as much."

His eyes narrowed. "If you knew this, then why are you here?"

"To try and end the strike. As a matter of fact, you gave me the idea."

He stared at her as though she'd taken leave of her senses. "*I* did?"

"You told me last night that where I led, the villagers would follow." Her smile turned impish. "So I just led the way to the fields. And you were right. It worked."

It took every ounce of willpower not to grab her by the shoulders and give her a good, hard shake. "Explain to me how this solves the basic problem."

"That's what I'm hoping you and I can do now."

He folded his arms across his chest. "I'm listening."

"You want me to leave the fields, right?"

"Of course I want you to leave."

"Perhaps we can reach a compromise. If you'd rehire Manuel—"

He shook his head, finally seeing the path her convoluted thinking had taken. "I cannot. It is a matter of honor."

"But—"

"It was a good try, *amada*," he said gently. "Unfortunately, it won't work."

Resentment crept into her gaze. "Only because you're unwilling to make it work."

He thrust a hand through his hair, thoroughly exasperated. "I refuse to argue the matter with you. Not while standing in the middle of a coffee field. And not while the entire citizenry of Milagro listens in."

"As well as your buyers?" she asked innocently, glancing at a point somewhere over his shoulder.

He restrained the urge to turn around. *Madre de Dios*! What more could go wrong? "You will pay for this, my love," he murmured for her ears alone. "I will see to it. Personally."

She inclined her head. "I look forward to the experience," came her impudent retort. "In the meantime, I'm afraid your wife will continue to pick coffee beans. It's a matter of honor for me, as well."

"Whose honor do you speak of?" This time he did grab hold of her, ignoring their fascinated spectators. He pulled her close so she would see his anger and determination. "Do you refer to the honor of *La Estrella*? She doesn't exist. What you are attempting will end in disaster. You will bring harm to the villagers and to yourself. End this now, Ella. Before it's too late."

"It's already too late."

"I can force you to leave," he warned. "I can physically remove you from this place."

"But you won't." She stepped back and he released her, his silence confirming her guess. "It may not be a perfect solution, Rafe. But at least the beans will get picked and the villagers will be paid. The rest is up to you." She started to leave, then hesitated.

He lifted an eyebrow. "Was there something else?"

"Are—are you all right?" she asked awkwardly, gesturing toward his bandaged hand.

A momentary softness gleamed within his silvery gaze. "I am fine. Thank you for your concern."

Still she hesitated. "You're sure?"

"Quite certain."

She sighed. "In that case, I'd better get back to work."

With that, she turned and headed into the fields. Picking up her basket, she fastened it around her waist and adjusted the brim of her hat to shade her face. Then she plucked a violently red cherry from amongst a cluster of green berries.

And as she led, so the people of Milagro followed.

Rafe approached the door to Ella's room. It was closed and he couldn't hear her moving around. He tapped on the wooden panel. When she didn't answer, he pushed it open. "Ella? It's time for dinner," he called.

And then he saw her.

Apparently working all day in the coffee fields had exhausted her, for she lay in the middle of the bed, sound asleep. She'd showered beforehand, wrapping herself in nothing more than a lightweight robe. A reluctant smile touched his mouth as he noticed her damp hair. She would have a job taming it when she eventually awoke. It fanned out behind her, the tumble of inky waves a sharp contrast to the crisp white pillowcase.

Unable to resist, he approached, staring down at her. She'd curled into a snug ball, her thin, silk robe pulled taut across her pertly rounded bottom and slender thighs. Her hands were folded beneath her chin, cushioned by her breasts, but he could still make out faintly stained fingernails. His smile grew.

Marvin had told him that she'd pried open a fair number of cherries. From what he could gather she'd repeatedly examined the twin beans inside, each time hoping to find a peaberry. If her rosy lips were any indication, she'd tasted her fair share of the sweet pulp, as well.

He crossed to her dresser and opened drawers at random until he found the one he sought. Removing a frothy silk nightgown, he crossed to the bed and eased her into his arms. Her lashes quivered for an instant and then she sighed, burrowing against him.

He held her for several long minutes, absorbing her warmth and sweet feminine fragrance. With a sigh of reluctance, he untied the robe and briskly stripped it from her. She was as beautiful as he remembered, full-breasted and narrow-waisted, her skin softer than a quetzal plume. He ignored the ache building in his loins and pulled the nightgown over her head. Just as he'd finished easing her arms through the appropriate openings, her eyelids fluttered and she blinked up at him.

"Hello," she said with a wide yawn.

"*Buenas noches, amada.*" To his relief, the lemon-colored silk drifted downward, concealing what tempted him almost beyond endurance.

Her head dipped to his shoulder again. "Did the buyers leave?" she asked sleepily.

"Long ago."

"Were they upset that your wife was working in the coffee fields?"

"Intrigued would be a more accurate description. They wondered if I were forcing you to pick the beans as a means of discipline."

She laughed, the sound low and husky and unbearably intimate. "The perfect excuse. I hope you took it."

"Tempting as it was, I did not."

Curiosity glittered in her gaze. "What did you tell them?"

"The truth."

"Oh," she murmured. "What was their reaction?"

"They were upset. Naturally, news of the strike did not please them."

"I'll bet."

He shifted her in his arms so her head rested more comfortably in the crook of his shoulder. "They requested that I bring in migrant laborers from Nicaragua to complete the job."

She tilted her head to look at him, alarm registering in her golden gaze. "Did you agree?"

"No. The villagers have traditionally picked *Esperanza* beans and they will continue to have that opportunity as long as I am owner of this *finca*."

"And when you're no longer the owner?"

He shrugged. "It is too early to say. I will do my best to protect them."

"I'm relieved to hear it." Another yawn caught her by surprise, blurring the end of her words. "Is it dinnertime? I guess I should get dressed."

"There's no point since I have just undressed you."

She glanced down, clearly amazed to discover herself wearing her nightgown. The tip of her tongue crept out to moisten her lips as she peeked up at him. "You undressed me . . . ?"

His gaze grew fiercely possessive. "Do you think I'd allow anyone else the pleasure?"

Disconcerted, her lashes flickered downward. "But dinner—"

"Chelita will bring you something on a tray."

"I can come down," she objected.

"Don't bother. You'd only end up falling asleep in your *olla de carne*."

"My what?"

"Your beef stew."

"But—"

"Do you intend to return to the coffee fields in the morning?" At her stubborn nod, he swept back the covers and deposited her between the sheets. "In that case, you will need your rest. Make sure you put on strong sun protection tomorrow. At this time of year, a little exposure can prove quite painful. If you need lotion, ask Chelita when she brings your meal."

Ella plumped the pillows behind her with unnecessary force. "Why do I feel like a child who's been put to bed early for acting naughty?"

"I can't think of a single reason," he retorted in an even voice. "Can you?"

She curled into a ball again, her lids drifting closed. "No," she muttered crossly. "I can't."

He brushed her hair from her cheek and feathered a kiss across her temple. "Good-night, *amada*," he whispered. "Dream of me."

By the time he'd reached the door, she'd fallen asleep again. He frowned in concern as he headed for the kitchen. This stalemate had to end or *La Estrella* was likely to collapse. And that wouldn't help anyone. He released his breath in an exasperated sigh, forced to concede the inevitable.

The time had come to have a serious talk with Manuel.

The next morning Ella dragged herself from bed and headed for the coffee fields before she could think of a good excuse to avoid it. She hurt. Badly. In fact, there wasn't a muscle in her body that didn't ache. Who would have thought picking coffee could be so difficult? Not that a few sore muscles would change her mind. Not a chance. She'd decided to attempt this particular miracle. And by heavens, she'd see it through to the bitter end. The villagers were waiting for her on the outskirts of the field. The moment she plucked the first cherry off the first tree, they immediately followed suit. Not five minutes passed, however, before nervous whispers warned that Rafe had once again come after her.

She turned to welcome him with a jaunty smile, praying that her exhaustion couldn't be seen on her face. Her prayers weren't answered. A frown crashed down on his brow.

"You look like hell, *amada*."

"And good morning to you, too."

"Fair warning," he leaned close to say. "Today this ends." Then in a louder voice, he announced, "I've come for my wife."

Before she could draw breath to ask what he meant, he yanked his switchblade from his pocket and flicked it open. In one easy move, he sliced through the harness.

The attached basket upended, spilling ripe beans into the dirt at her feet.

"Rafe!"

His name ended in a panicked shriek as he picked her up. Tossing her over his shoulder like a sack of potatoes, he spoke in rapid Spanish to the workers. To her utter astonishment, they burst into loud cheers. Twisting around to look, her hat snagged on a nearby branch. It was lifted neatly off her head, while her loosened hair tumbled free, clouding her vision. Planting her hands on the solid wall of his back, she shoved upward.

"What's going on?" she demanded furiously, shaking her hair back from her face.

His only response was to wrap one arm around the back of her knees and bounce her to a more secure spot on his shoulder. Her breath left her lungs in an audible gasp. Catching hold of the back of his belt, she hung on for dear life as he strode from the fields. Once they were well out of view of the villagers, he dropped her to her feet. She staggered and he caught her elbow while she steadied herself.

"You want to explain what all that was about?" she questioned grumpily. She attempted to bring some sort of order to her hair, but soon gave it up as a lost cause.

"That was about saving face."

"I figured as much." She glanced back at the fields. "Why did they cheer?"

"Because I ended the strike."

She swiveled to look at him. "You— You're not selling the *finca*?" she questioned hopefully. "You've changed your mind?"

He shook his head. "I warned you it wasn't that simple. I fired Manuel for a very good reason. I'm not about to rehire him just because you've been rash enough to step in where you don't belong."

"Then how did you end the strike?"

A cold smile touched his mouth. "As a matter of fact, you gave me the idea that night at dinner."

"*I* did?"

"You said that you'd hire Chelita if I fired her." He inclined his head in response to her dawning comprehension. "It seemed fitting to turn the tables on you. I may not be in a position to hire Manuel, since I'm the one who fired him. But you can. The distinction isn't lost on the workers. It appeases them so they're willing to return to work—"

"While still allowing you to save face." She nodded ruefully. It wasn't quite what she'd hoped to achieve, but it was a start. "What am I supposed to do with Manuel? I don't really need an employee."

Rafe shrugged. "That's your problem. But in future, I'd appreciate your staying out of my business. No more miracles. Are we clear?"

Her brows drew together. "I'm not sure we are."

"Then allow me to make it clear. I leave for San José within the hour. A problem with the sale of *Esperanza* has cropped up and must be dealt with. Don't look so hopeful," he was quick to add, accurately interpreting her reaction. "The problem is nothing that a few days' discussion won't correct."

She smiled sweetly. "I'm sorry to hear that."

"I'm sure you are." His expression might have been carved from stone. "While I'm gone I suggest you give your future plans careful consideration. Stop worrying about matters you can't change and start worrying about matters you can."

"Meaning?"

"Your own position is somewhat precarious at the moment—far more so than the villagers. At least they have my protection. You do not, as you discovered last night. I recommend you think about ways to correct that."

"You're referring to the agreement you want from my parents."

"Yes."

"One conversation can straighten that out," she assured him calmly.

"I'm relieved to hear it." He waited a beat before adding, "We'll have that conversation on my return. Now are we clear?"

"As crystal."

"Excellent."

And with that, he turned and—once again—walked away.

Over the next several days, she considered what Rafe had said. But it didn't change her mind. It just made her more determined than ever to find a way to get through to him, as well as to find out why he was so hell-bent on selling *Esperanza*. Once she discovered the answer to that, perhaps she could prevent the sale and help the villagers. And then there was Shayne. Although Ella knew she couldn't wave a magic wand and make Chaz McIntyre reappear, she just might be able to give some assistance in another area.

Shayne's mosaics.

Manuel had told her about an art gallery in San José that specialized in unique artworks by local artisans. It sounded perfect for what she hoped to accomplish. If she showed a few pieces to the proprietor, maybe an expert could convince Shayne that her talent shouldn't be wasted. Unfortunately, in order to put her plan into motion, she needed to go into the city while Rafe was away.

It took hours of arguing to convince Manuel to help. "You don't understand," he protested. "I cannot bring you back. I have to return to school."

"I can drive myself back. I'll watch the route we take—"

He shook his head. "It's not that simple. The mountain roads can be very confusing. And they're dangerous. There are rock slides. We get sudden downpours where entire sections of road wash away. Not to mention the potholes. If something happened to you—"

"Nothing will happen. Not if you draw a map and not if I'm careful. Please, Manuel. It's important. I wouldn't ask you to do this if it were just for me. But it's for Shayne. Or do you want her to spend the rest of her life working as an accountant?"

"What's wrong with being an accountant?"

"Nothing, if that's what Shayne really wanted. Can you honestly say it is?"

"No," he admitted. "Creating mosaics has been her obsession since she was a teenager. She even had a few commissions before..." His shrug spoke volumes. "Just the other day, when she thought no one was watching, she sketched a new design for her portfolio."

His words confirmed what Ella already suspected. "Then you'll help?"

He sighed. "I will help. But if anything goes wrong, you could work in the coffee fields until doomsday and still not salvage my job a second time."

That gave her pause. She wouldn't want to do anything to harm Manuel's future. And though that future wasn't picking coffee berries, she didn't doubt Rafe had a long reach. Not to mention a propensity for vengeance. "I promise. I'll be very careful."

And she was. The entire way to San José the next morning, she paid close attention to the route. Even after they arrived in the city, she reviewed the map Manuel had drawn and thoroughly familiarized herself with it. Next, they located the art gallery.

"The owner is away on a buying trip," explained the assistant, a friendly young woman, with an appealing smile. "But I'd be happy to show him your mosaics when he returns."

"I can leave them with you?" Ella asked. "You wouldn't mind?"

"Not at all." She examined them appreciatively. "They're stunning. I'm certain *Señor* Jiménez will be most impressed."

After leaving a phone number and address where Shayne could be reached, Manuel drove to the outskirts of the university. He insisted on going over the map one last time before he was satisfied that she could safely find her way to Milagro.

"I'll start back right away," she assured him. "Don't worry. I'll be home well before dark."

"It won't matter. Your husband will have my head for this regardless," he predicted gloomily. "Even if it is for a good cause."

Ella grinned. "Well, Chelita will appreciate the effort you've taken even if Rafe doesn't."

Once again dusky color tinged his cheekbones. "*Hasta luego, Estrella. Vaya con Dios.*"

"The same to you. And...thank you, Manuel."

Taking a deep breath, Ella put the car in gear and pulled into traffic. To her relief, the trip progressed without incident. She took her time, managing to avoid most of the potholes she came across and all of the oncoming cars. They passed at such high rates of speed she suspected they'd end up finding their way down the mountain by the fastest possible route—off a cliff and straight to the bottom. To her relief, the kamikaze traffic vanished once she turned onto the side road that led to Milagro.

Two thirds of the way home, she skirted a pile of branches dumped in the middle of the road. And rounding the next curve she ran into trouble.

Serious trouble.

CHAPTER NINE

RAFE stood by the side of the road, leaning against his car, a jacket hooked over one shoulder. Ella immediately applied the brakes and pulled in behind him. He stared for a moment, then shook his head and walked toward her.

"Why am I not surprised to see you?" he asked, resting his forearms on the edge of her open window.

She couldn't help smiling. "I don't know. Why?"

"Perhaps it's because I so frequently find you where you don't belong."

"Well ... Maybe you should just change your opinion of where I do—or rather, don't—belong."

"I have reached a similar conclusion," he admitted wryly. "Is there any point in asking what you're doing here?"

"I'd rather discuss what *you're* doing," she replied candidly.

"Broken water pump. I've been waiting for a Good Samaritan to come to my rescue."

Her smile grew. "And here I am. The answer to your prayers."

"The answer to many prayers, I fear," he said with resignation.

She thought better of responding to that one. "If you're willing to drive, I'd be happy to give you a lift."

He raised an eyebrow. "Don't you like our roads, *amada*?"

What would be the most delicate way of phrasing her reply? "No."

"In that case I'd be happy to offer my services. Let me get my luggage and briefcase and we can be on our way."

He returned a moment later and dumped his bags and suit coat onto the backseat. Climbing behind the steering wheel, he shot her a curious glance. "You still haven't told me what you're doing here." Pulling onto the road, he carefully skirted his abandoned car, the narrow lane leaving little room to spare.

Around the next bend she spotted another pile of branches. "I saw those on the last curve," she commented. "Why would someone just dump them in the middle of the road, like that?"

"I put them there to indicate a hazard ahead. It's a common practice. And you haven't answered my question."

She hadn't expected to successfully divert him. Still, it had been worth a try. "I went into San José."

He frowned. "On your own?"

"No, Manuel drove me." His frown grew fiercer and she hastened to emphasize, "As my employee, he could hardly refuse my request for a driver. Although to give him credit, he tried."

"I suspect if he hadn't consented, you'd have gone on your own," Rafe guessed shrewdly.

"True enough. He needed to go back to the university, so we drove in together."

"Leaving you to return to Milagro by yourself?"

She took instant exception to the implied criticism. "He drew a very detailed map and went over it several times." Her mouth tightened. "I'm a twenty-six-year-old woman, Rafe. Not a child. I'm perfectly capable of driving myself from point A to point B without a man along to help."

He let that pass. "What were you so anxious to accomplish in San José that it couldn't wait until I'd concluded my business?"

"Actually, I didn't think you'd be willing to take me," she confessed.

Comprehension dawned. "Once I knew what you wanted, you mean?"

"Yes."

"And the purpose for this trip was... what?"

She shot him a nervous glance. She'd been most concerned about his reaction to this part of the story. Best to get it over with quickly. "I took several of Shayne's mosaic pieces to an art gallery for an expert opinion on their quality."

"Performing more miracles, *Estrella*?" he inquired with surprising tolerance.

"Just a very tiny one."

Before he could say anything more, the car gave an odd coughing sound. Muttering a curse, Rafe pulled to the side of the road once again. With a tired wheeze, the engine died.

"What's wrong? What happened?" Ella asked.

"Give me a moment to see." He attempted to restart the car, without success. Next, he opened the door to get out, then paused. "Ah... *amada*?"

She didn't care for the tenor of his voice. "Yes?"

"When you were busy being this independent twenty-six-year-old woman capable of driving herself from point A to point B... Did you by any chance check the fuel level?"

She cringed. "We're out of gas?"

"Yes, we're out of gas!"

"Oh."

"Oh? That's all you have to say?"

"Um. I'm glad you're here to keep me company?"

He climbed from the car and slammed the door closed. "Sit tight and don't move."

"Where are you going?"

"I'm going to put more branches in the road."

"I can help."

He spun around and strode back to the car. "No. You can't help. And, no. You won't help. You will sit without moving so much as an inch. Understand? The way our luck is running, you're likely to gather up some man-zanillo branches and poison yourself."

She folded her arms across her chest and glared. "Even you couldn't be that lucky. Besides, they only grow by the ocean and you know it."

He poked his head through the open window. "First of all, there would be nothing lucky about losing you to the 'tree of death,'" he informed her in no uncertain terms. "And second, I don't care where it grows. With your propensity for sticking your nose where it doesn't belong, you'd manage to find one. Now don't move."

Ten minutes later he returned to the car. "It may be a while. I don't suppose you have any bottled water?"

"Actually I do. Manuel insisted," she informed him, hoping to score a few points on the student's behalf. "I also have a thermos of left-over coffee and a bag full of Tico snacks I couldn't live without. Or so Manuel informed me."

Rafe picked up the large bag she indicated and looked inside. "I may have to forgive his lapse in judgment in taking you to San José. He has made some excellent choices. We won't starve, that's for certain."

"What's in there?" She peeked over his shoulder. "I haven't even checked."

He shifted toward her side of the seat so she'd have a better view. "Are you hungry?"

"Very."

"Well, we have *tortas* and *chorreados*."

"Which are?"

"*Tortas* are a bread containing meat and vegetables. And *chorreados* are a corn pancake." He rummaged through the bag. "It would seem Manuel has a sweet tooth. Half the bag has been filled with *cajeta, pañuelos y tapitas.*"

"All right. I give up. What's a *cajeta*?"

"It's fudge."

"And *pañ*—"

"*Pañuelos.* The literal translation is handkerchief. But it's a pastry."

"And *tapitas*?"

"A small chocolate wrapped in foil." He gave her a lazy smile. "Is this a Spanish lesson? Perhaps there are more words you'd like to learn."

His question sparked her curiosity and she slowly nodded. "As a matter of fact there are." She gazed at him intently. "What does *esperanza* mean? I keep forgetting to ask."

His jaw tightened, his amusement vanishing with frightening speed. Clearly, he hadn't expected that particular question. "It means hope," he said without expression.

She stared at him, stunned. "Your *finca* is named hope?"

"Not from choice."

"That I can believe." Her curiosity grew. "And the town? What is *Milagro* in English?"

"Miracle."

She drew a shaky breath. "And *amada*?"

He gazed out the front windshield and shrugged. "It is a form of endearment. One not often used." He tossed the bag into her lap. "I thought you were hungry. Have the *cajeta*. It's quite good."

"*Amada*," she repeated deliberately, shoving the bag aside. "What does it mean?"

His voice was so low and rough, she had to strain to catch his response. "Beloved." He thrust his hand into his pocket. "What the *hell* have I done with my cigarettes?"

"You threw them out, remember?" she murmured, badly shaken.

"The day you arrived. How could I forget?"

"Don't change the subject." She touched his shoulder, drawing his gaze. "All this time, that's what you've been calling me? Beloved?"

"You must have realized it was a form of endearment," he said testily.

"Not really."

"What did you think I'd been calling you?"

"I don't know. Dark-haired woman... Most annoying one... Silly twit. I was afraid to ask."

Amusement turned his eyes to points of silver light. "Silly twit?"

"I think I prefer beloved."

"I would hope so."

She snuggled closer, dropping her head to his shoulder. "I missed you," she confessed.

"And I, you. It has been a long few days." His fingers grazed her cheek. "I trust you've stayed out of the coffee fields while I've been gone?"

"Yes. Have you changed your mind about selling the *finca*?"

"No."

"Is it because you can't bear to live on a ranch called 'hope' outside a town called 'miracle'?"

"I have lived there for a good portion of my life." His hand shifted from her cheek to ruffle her hair. "I would not sell my home for such a trivial reason."

"Then why?"

He hesitated. "I'm doing it for Shayne's sake," he finally said, answering the question that had plagued her since she'd arrived.

"*Shayne*?"

"You aren't the only one who has seen changes in her," he responded indirectly. "She isn't the same girl she was five years ago. Everything she ever held dear, she has pushed away."

"Including you?"

He didn't spare himself. "To a certain extent. Yes."

"Because you took her from Chaz McIntyre?"

"There could be no other reason." He released his breath in a ragged sigh. "I have tortured myself over that decision for years, wondering if I made a mistake. I've analyzed it again and again and each time I come to the same conclusion. She was a child who'd only known this man for a few short hours. To have left her in his care would have been wrong."

"Why did she marry him? Do you know?"

"Yes. I know." He gave her a straight look. "She wanted the fairy tale. She wanted your life, *amada*. A life she'd never had."

"My life?" Ella repeated, taken aback. "But she lived a fairy tale existence of her own. Why would she think mine better than the one she already had?"

He hesitated. "Her life was not a fairy tale."

"I realize you lost your parents, but—"

"Our father and her mother were killed in a boating accident when I was sixteen. Shayne was three."

She stared at him, stunned. "I hadn't realized you were so young. Were there relatives to help?"

"No."

"But... What in the world did you do?"

"What could I do? I tried to keep our life together, to take care of the coffee *finca*, to take care of my little sister, to protect all those who depended on me." He shrugged as though it didn't matter. But she knew better. "I failed. I lost everything—the estate, what little money I inherited from my parents. But worst of all, I lost Shayne."

Ella recalled the conversation she'd had with her father on Christmas night. He'd said that Rafe had once lost control of his life. That he fought an ongoing battle to ensure it never happen again. This must be what her father had been referring to. Though how he'd uncovered the story, she couldn't begin to guess.

"What do you mean, you lost her?" she asked gently. "What happened to Shayne?"

"When I realized I could no longer care for her, that soon we'd be without a home or enough food to survive, I called my stepmother's sister. Jackie lived in Florida. And though she'd been violently opposed to the marriage, I decided to take a chance, thinking that under the circumstances she might help."

"I assumed Shayne's mother was Tico," Ella said in surprise.

"No. Ironic, is it not? I am but one quarter native, Shayne not at all."

"So, did Jackie come?"

"She came. And then she left with Shayne."

It took a moment to absorb the significance. "Just Shayne?" Ella asked softly.

Again came that careless shrug. "We weren't related, Jackie and I. Therefore she was under no obligation to help 'a filthy Tico peasant.'"

"Oh, Rafe. I'm so sorry."

"Save your sympathy. It was not I who needed it."

"Your sister...?"

He stared through the front windshield as though peering into the distant past, lost in dark memories. "She was gone from my life, but not a day went by that I didn't think about her, wonder and worry about whether I'd done the right thing by giving her to Jackie."

"What else could you have done?"

"That question has haunted me from the moment I placed Shayne in that woman's arms."

"What did you do after they left?"

"I worked for the next ten years rebuilding my finances. When the price of coffee bottomed out in the mid-eighties, *Esperanza* came on the market again and I bought it. Soon afterward, money was no longer a problem." His mouth tightened. "So I went looking for Shayne. I had to make sure I'd done the right thing by giving her to Jackie."

She dreaded asking the next question. "What did you find?"

"That I'd made a terrible mistake. I gather feeding and clothing and raising a child—even one partly her own flesh and blood—was not how Jackie wished to spend her life. She made certain that Shayne paid every day for having been 'rescued' from her previous existence." He closed his eyes. "My sweet *hermanita* had gone from a bright extroverted child to a shy, nervous teenager starving for love and affection."

Tears stung Ella's eyes. Poor Shayne. "What happened then?"

"Jackie sold my sister to me."

"*Sold* her?"

"Sold her like a commodity. I took Shayne back to Costa Rica and I swore I'd protect her from that day on. I succeeded. I succeeded, that is, until one terrible night five years ago."

"The Cinderella Ball."

He nodded. "She was so susceptible to its allure. It offered all that she'd been denied as a child. Love, happiness and happily-ever-after. How could she resist such a temptation?"

"She couldn't," Ella acknowledged.

"Perhaps she'd have been better off if I'd left her with McIntyre. But she was so young. And I had failed to protect her from Jackie. I couldn't fail again."

"I'm sure Chaz didn't know her real age."

"To his credit, I don't think so, either."

"You've explained about Shayne. But you still haven't told me what that has to do with selling the *finca*."

He frowned. "As long as *Esperanza* is her home, she will continue to hide from life. You have seen her, have seen the changes in her. She is a woman who has lost her direction."

"I thought she was studying to become an accountant."

"She studies so she can help me. It's as though she's paying penitence for a sin she never committed. I once offered to finance whatever dream she cared to fulfill. But she will take nothing from me. It's as though she's lost her love for life."

"And the funds from the sale of *Esperanza*? Why would she accept that when she wouldn't take the other money you offered?"

"I never told her I'd lost the estate. All she knows is that it was left to both of us equally on the death of our parents—which is true. She'll consider herself entitled to those funds. At least, I hope so. Even if she does not, she'll be forced out into the world."

"You won't be able to protect her in that world," Ella felt obligated to caution.

He rubbed the crease furrowing his brow. "A seventeen-year-old teenager needs adult protection to avoid a painful fall. I am forced to concede, however, that a twenty-three-year-old woman should be permitted to stumble once or twice. By skinning an occasional knee, she'll be in a better position to protect her own children when the time comes."

"But it's difficult to let go, isn't it?"

"Perhaps the most difficult thing I've ever done."

"That's why you weren't upset when you found out I'd taken her mosaics to the art gallery."

"Yes." His gaze held a warning. "She'll be angry when she discovers what you've done."

"At least if she's angry, she'll be feeling something."

A car horn blared just then. They looked up to see Marvin's cab skidding around the curve toward them. He honked again in greeting, then stopped in the middle of the road. "It is a good thing I have come along, yes?" he called.

Rafe climbed from the car. "A very good thing, my friend. Are you here by luck or by design?"

"A bit of both. Manuel left instructions. He said that if *La Estrella* didn't show up by midafternoon, I was to come looking for her. Just in case." He grinned. "It was a good plan, yes?"

"It was an excellent plan," Ella said dryly. "Thank you."

"*De nada*," Marvin rubbed his hands together. "So... What is the problem?"

"We're out of gas," Rafe told him succinctly.

Marvin's gaze switched from one to the other. He struggled to conceal his amusement and failed. "*No problema*," he said. " I will have you on your way *muy rapido*."

"I'd like to take Ella to see the sunset at *Abrazo de Amante*. Do you have enough gas to spare?"

"*Por supuesto*. It would be my pleasure." In no time, Marvin had the gas syphoned from one tank to the other. "I will warn Chelita of your late arrival," he offered when he'd finished.

"I'd appreciate that," Rafe said.

"And I have something else you might appreciate." Marvin opened the trunk of his car and pulled out a large folded blanket, tossing it to Rafe. "Take this and enjoy your embrace."

Color tinted Ella's cheekbones. "Why did he say that?" she demanded.

"*Abrazo de Amante*. It means 'lover's embrace.' He was just making a little joke."

"Oh." She slanted another look in Rafe's direction. "Why is it called that?"

He smiled cryptically as he started the engine. "You'll see."

Further down the road, he turned onto a small side track that dipped back down the mountainside. It was little more than two ruts slicing through the thick foliage. He drove carefully, allowing her to get a good look at the variety of birds that winged across their path.

"That's a motmot," he said, pointing to a bird whose long electric-blue tail flicked back and forth like the pendulum of a clock. "And a pair of toucans are hiding in that tree there."

At the next turn, he pulled to a stop so she could watch the noisy antics of several howler monkeys shaking the branches overhead. But the most breathtaking sight of all was the brief glimpse she caught of the spectacular Morpho butterfly, its cobalt wings flashing like iridescent jewels against the vivid green canopy.

They rounded a final curve and she stared in astonishment. A huge rock pool spread out before them, fed by a spring. Steam rose from the glassy surface, wafting off the water to fog the surrounding forest. It was primeval, stirring a response that felt as ancient and elemental as the jungle itself.

"*Abrazo de Amante*," Rafe said softly, turning off the engine.

"Now I understand why Marvin gave you the blanket."

He left the car and she followed, unable to drag her eyes from temptation. She itched to shed her sticky clothes and climb into the hot tub nature had so kindly provided.

Drifting closer to the pool, she asked, "Can we... Can we go in?"

He came to stand behind her, so close his breath stirred her hair. "Take off your blouse," he directed, the warmth of his body radiating along the length of her spine.

She didn't hesitate. Continuing to stare at the steaming water, she lifted a hand to work the buttons. One by one they slipped through the holes. When she'd finished, she shrugged the lightweight cotton off her shoulders. It never hit the ground. Rafe snagged it as it fluttered earthward.

"Your skirt."

He didn't move any closer, but simply waited. Keeping her back to him, she obediently lowered the side zip. Still without actually touching her, he bunched her skirt and slip in his fists and pulled them both to her waist. Then he swept them over her head before stepping back once more.

It was the strangest striptease she'd ever done—the only striptease she'd ever done. Erotic and yet innocent. Touching without touching. It made her keenly aware of her own sexuality, that she was removing her clothing for the pleasure of a man. The fact that that man happened to be her husband made it all the more tantalizing. The fact that they'd never made love before, made the tension almost unbearable.

"What next?" she whispered.

"Your bra."

She unhooked the scrap of white lace. Lowering her arms to her sides, she crooked her elbows slightly so the straps caught there. He reached around her, his hand so close to her skin, she could feel the heat he generated. He leaned in, his warm breath teasing across her shoulder and down the slopes of her breasts, furling the peaks into tight little rosebuds. He hooked his finger around one silky strap and waited until she dropped her arms. The lace fell into his grasp.

"And now?" she asked.

"There's only one thing left."

"Do I take it off or leave it on?"

His voice grated. "Take it off."

This would be the most difficult part of all. She closed her eyes, debating whether or not she should end the game now. Never in her life had she felt so vulnerable. But her decision boiled down to two simple words. Trust. And love. It was Rafe standing behind her. The man she loved with all her heart and trusted with her very soul. He'd never hurt her, despite what he'd threatened. And she wanted him, wanted to be his wife in fact as well as name.

Without further hesitation, she kicked off her sandals and slipped her thumbs into the elastic waistband, inching the lightweight silk down her hips. She could hear the sharp intake of his breath followed by the ragged release, sensed he was teetering on the knife's edge between restraint and raw instinct. Once her underpants had slid past her thighs, they floated to the ground. She took a step forward, leaving them behind.

She smiled, knowing he couldn't see her expression, and lifted her hands to her hair, removing the clip that restrained it. With a quick shake, the strands tumbled free, veiling her neck and shoulders in a thick dark curtain.

She glanced behind her then, allowing him to witness her smile. Before he could act on the savage need burning in his eyes, she darted toward the pool. She hesitated for an instant at the rocky rim, testing the temperature with her toe. It was perfect. She slipped in, the warmth of the water sheathing her like a velvet glove. *Abrazo de Amante*. The name made perfect sense to her now.

"Feel good?" he called to her, his voice stark with desire.

"It's unbelievable."

"Have you ever gone swimming in the rough before?"

"Never. It's—it's . . ."

A hard grin slashed across his face. "Yes, it is."

The pool was deep, well over her head, and full of large black rocks. The heated water felt like a lover's hand, swirled over her breasts and between her legs in the most sensuous caress she'd ever experienced. She drifted toward the center, watching Rafe.

He hadn't taken his gaze from her. At a distance his eyes appeared black instead of gray, but there was no mistaking the intent registering in that scorching look. He wanted her. Badly. Every line of his body, every ripple of compact muscle underscored that desire. He swiftly shed his shirt and shoes, and in one easy move, ripped his belt from the loops. Then he reached for his zipper.

A light breeze stirred the steam so that warm spray kissed her skin and caught in her hair, sparkling like stardust. Kicking lightly to one side of the pool, she dove deep into the heated heart. It was sheer bliss. She glided underwater toward the edge closest to Rafe, hoping to surface and surprise him. But as she started up, her hair snagged in a narrow crevice between the pile of rocks.

She tugged, expecting the strands to pull loose. Instead, they held fast. She tugged again, harder this time, the first glimmer of panic radiating through her subconscious. But no matter what she tried, she couldn't work her way free. She couldn't even get enough leverage to plant her feet against the slippery rocks and use her leg muscles to rip the hair from its anchor. Her chest burned, lending urgency to her actions. In sheer desperation, she kicked toward the surface as hard as she could, stretching out her hand in an effort to break the plane of the water and alert Rafe. Her trapped hair yanked her backward.

She was going to die. She knew it. Her mouth opened in a silent scream and water poured in.

CHAPTER TEN

RAFE placed his clothing on the front seat of the car and turned, staring across the pool with a frown. Something was wrong. Very wrong. He could feel it. And then it hit him.

He couldn't see Ella.

Driven by pure instinct, he reached back into the car. Snatching his switchblade free of his trouser's pocket, he pivoted, sprinting flat-out for the pool. What he found there turned his blood to ice. Ella's hair had become caught in the underwater rocks and she was trying frantically to pull the strands loose.

Flicking open his knife, he dove to her side. Her hands were in his way and he yanked them clear. Panicking, she fought back, too desperate for air to understand his intent. Finally he wrapped an arm around her, locking her flailing limbs tight against his body. Dragging her as far from the deadly rocks as possible, he slashed his knife through her trapped hair. Not wasting another second, he kicked toward salvation.

She tried to inhale the minute they broke the surface. Instead she choked, the water filling her lungs making breathing an impossibility. Rafe tossed his knife onto the rocks and heaved himself from the pool, hanging on to her with one hand. Reaching down, he hauled her up and into his arms. She collapsed against him and he bent her at the waist, squeezing her ribs until she'd dispelled enough water to breathe.

Weak tears spilled from her eyes. "Rafe," she whispered hoarsely. "Oh, Rafe. Hold me."

"I'm here, *amada*. I have you." He cradled her more tightly in his arms, sweeping her hair from her face. "Easy, *pobrecita*. Take it easy."

She fought to speak. "I thought I was going to die."

"I would not let that happen," he said simply.

"I didn't think you saw." She shuddered. "I couldn't reach you. I couldn't let you know that I needed you."

His mouth caressed her temple. "I knew. Somehow I knew." She shivered again and he started to stand. "You're cold. Let me get the blanket."

Tears welled up in her eyes again. "No! Don't leave me."

"Just for a moment," he soothed. "I'll be right back."

Even the few seconds it took to reach the car and grab the blanket seemed an eternity. As soon as he returned, he wrapped the heavy cotton around them both and sat with her on the edge of the rocks. In time her shivers eased and her breathing grew more relaxed.

"Come," he said at last. "Let's get dressed and go home."

"No, not home. I'd rather go back in the water."

Her request caught him off guard. "I don't think that's a good idea."

"I know it sounds crazy, but... This is too beautiful a place to leave with such bad memories." She gazed at him, her eyes vibrant bits of gold. "Please, Rafe."

He couldn't argue with her, not after what she'd just experienced. If she had the courage to return to the water, who was he to object? "Then come," he said. He drew her toward the rim of the pool, absorbing the shiver that rippled through her as they paused at the edge.

And then her fear evaporated, absolute faith implicit in the glance she sent him. "Take me in with you."

"Do not look at me like that, *amada*," he demanded.

"Like what?"

"With such trust."

"But I do trust you. With my life, as it turns out."

His mouth tightened. "You should not."

To his irritation, she gave a soft, knowing laugh. Gritting his teeth, he helped her into the water, never allowing her to drift further than arm's length. But there was a steep price to pay for such close care. Every few minutes she brushed against him. Her lush bottom drifted over his hip. Her full, ripe breasts danced along his forearm. With unerring accuracy, her unguarded foot found the taut length of his thigh. When he felt the pebbled tip of her breast scrape across his back, he could stand no more.

"We should get out before I do something we both regret," he said, barely restraining a groan.

"What is it you think I'll regret?" She smiled. It was a revealing sort of smile and understanding crashed in on him.

"You play a dangerous game," he informed her tightly.

"And you don't play at all."

It was the last straw. With a guttural snarl, he lunged. Wrapping her in an unrelenting hold, he kicked to the far side of the pool.

"You have been begging for this."

"Since the night we were married," she confirmed without hesitation. "Are you finally going to give it to me?"

He closed his eyes, his anger dissipating as swiftly as it had emerged. "Yes, *amada*. Since it's what I want, too, it will be all too easy to give you what you wish."

Ella hesitated, catching her lower lip between her teeth. "If I say I love you, will you leave like you did on our wedding night?"

He shook his head, but deep furrows carved a path from his cheekbones to the tense line of his jaw. "I don't have that much control. Not anymore."

"In that case..." Cupping his face, she took his mouth in a tender kiss. "I love you, Rafe. Please make me your wife."

"I cannot give you all that you ask," he whispered. "But I will give you all that I have."

Mist rising off the pool dewed his hair with diamond droplets, matching the silver glitter of his eyes. She splayed her hand across his collarbone, tracing the ragged scars she found there. With a murmur of regret, she bent and kissed each individual mark of valor. His muscles knotted beneath her fingers and she followed the taut lines down his chest to the corrugated surface of his belly.

"Do not go any further," he warned roughly. "Or this moment will end before it has begun."

"Tell me what you want."

"Why don't I show you, instead." He slid his hands beneath her arms and lifted. His breath came rapidly, hot against her damp skin. "You are so beautiful. The most beautiful woman I have ever known."

Water sluiced downward, beading on the tips of her breasts. She whispered his name, half in encouragement, half in protest. With a low groan, he caught the tears of moisture with his tongue. She gripped his shoulders, her eyes drifting shut. Then his mouth closed on her, each tiny love bite more pleasing than the last.

"Good?" he murmured, his jaw a delicious abrasion against her sensitive skin.

"Do you need to ask?"

"I can make it better."

She laughed, the sound low and husky. "I don't think that's possible."

"You will see. Grab the rock above you, *amada*."

She looked up. A fingerlike outcropping jutted directly overhead and she reached for it, latching onto the rough surface so she hung half in, half out of the water. Her weight pulled her taut and he took full advantage of the exposed landscape, wandering over creamy hillocks and into delicate hollows, exploring rich deltas and moist caverns. And always he drove her. Past curiosity. Past budding desire. Relentlessly pushing her toward an all-consuming desperation for fulfillment.

Her breathing grew labored, her body heavy with need. "I can't hold on any longer."

"Wrap your legs around my waist and let go."

She did as he requested and he caught her as she fell, slowing her descent. Palming her bottom, he sheathed himself within her, burning heat melding into innocent warmth. When he could go no further, he lifted her again, starting the slow, stormy slide all over.

She trembled helplessly, filled with such joy and wonder that tears flooded her eyes. This was what she'd waited for, refusing to settle for less, knowing that it wouldn't be right without Rafe. As though sensing her thoughts, he whispered tender words, striving to make each moment sweeter than the last. Bit by bit their pace increased until the hot water washed over and around them, slapping, splashing, churning. And then came the moment that fused them into one, shattering in its impact.

In that instant, Ella felt as though anything was possible. The villagers would receive the prosperity and happiness they'd long awaited. Shayne would find satisfaction and contentment through her mosaic work. The *finca* wouldn't have to be sold. And, Rafe... Rafe would end his vendetta and allow love into his life.

At long last, she'd receive the magic of the Cinderella Ball. And with that magic, she'd discover happily-ever-after in the arms of the man she loved with all her heart and soul.

Rafe and Ella returned to *Esperanza* just as the sun set. "Why don't I ask Chelita to fix a salad for us?" he suggested, wrapping an arm around her shoulders. "After working our way through Manuel's bag of snacks, I'm not very hungry."

"I'm not, either. A salad sounds perfect." She paused within the cool shelter of the entranceway, her quiet voice amplified by the slate flooring. "I'll go shower, then meet you in the dining room. All right?"

Chelita appeared just then. "*Disculpe, Señor*," she said nervously.

"Yes?"

She spared a swift glance for Ella. "*El padre de la Señora está aquí. Quiere hablar con usted solo. Solamente usted.*"

"*Adónde?*"

"*En la oficina.*"

He frowned. "Thank you, Chelita. I'll deal with it."

"Is something wrong?" Ella asked. She'd recognized a word or two of the housekeeper's rapid-fire Spanish, but not enough to follow the conversation.

"Go ahead and shower. I have some business to attend to." He hesitated. "Perhaps you should come to my office once you've changed."

"There's something wrong, isn't there?"

"That's what I'm going to find out."

"Why don't I come now?"

He shook his head, his expression adamant. "Give me a moment first. It may be nothing."

She didn't argue. But an inexplicable fear seized her. In sudden need of reassurance, she caught his face between her palms and tugged him toward her. He didn't require any prompting, but covered her mouth in an ardent kiss. One hand bunched in the damp curls of her hair, his other followed the length of her spine, molding her against him. She felt his desire return, felt the desperate need reassert itself.

"We can't," he muttered.

"I know." She sighed, catching his bottom lip between her teeth and tugging gently. "Thank you for today. Maybe tomorrow—"

"Do not say it, *amada*." He closed his eyes, deep lines slashing along the sides of his mouth. "Today might be all I can give you."

"I don't believe that," she protested. "I won't believe it."

He started to speak, then shook his head. "Go and shower. I was wrong to say anything. This isn't the appropriate time."

She shivered, suddenly cold. "I hope that time never comes."

He didn't respond, but stood motionless and silent, his eyes an unreadable sooty gray. Standing on tiptoe, she planted a quick kiss along the taut line of his jaw and headed for her room. She didn't rush her shower. Although part of her wanted to hurry back to Rafe, a more rational part urged caution. Something had happened in the entranceway. Something that had changed his attitude toward her. And she wasn't in any hurry to discover what that might be. She needed a second to herself. A brief moment in which to relive the past several hours. A brief moment in which to believe that dreams could come true.

Once she'd finished dressing, she made her way to Rafe's office. After knocking, she pushed open the door. Rafe sat behind his desk. And leaning across it, speaking in irate tones, was her father. Clearly, they hadn't heard her knock.

"...idea what you're doing!" Donald was asserting.

Rafe stared at him coldly. "I know precisely what I'm doing."

"Dad," she said in astonishment. "I didn't know you were here."

They both looked up at the same instant, conflicting expressions on their faces. Her father looked furious. Rafe appeared resigned. "Come in, *amada*. And close the door."

"I don't want her involved in this," Donald protested.

"It is far too late for that."

She glanced from one to the other. "What's going on?"

"Go ahead," Rafe ordered. "Tell her."

After a momentary hesitation, Donald said, "It's a financial matter. It has to do with our mortgage. It comes up for renewal soon and..." He shrugged in resignation. "There's no easy way to say this, so I'll be blunt. The company who owns the note—the Phoenix Corporation—won't renew it. And the banks I've approached have been less than helpful."

Ella fought to control her alarm. "The banks weren't helpful in the first place. That's why you went to Phoenix. When does this note come due?"

"In three days."

She spared a brief glance for her husband. "What does this have to do with Rafe?"

"I've come to ask his advice."

Her father was being evasive, she could tell. "Why *his* advice?"

"If I can't get the loan extended, our only option is to sell the house."

"*Sell*..." She turned to Rafe. "You have to help."

"What is it you'd like me to do?" he inquired politely.

"I don't know. Come up with something!"

"Ella—" her father began.

Rafe cut in. "I would think the funds generated from these Cinderella Balls would be more than sufficient to meet several years' worth of loan payments."

"They would," Ella said impatiently. "If my parents kept the profit instead of donating it to charity."

He frowned. "Charity?"

"You didn't think we kept the money, did you? Look, could we get back to the matter at hand? What if you talked to this Phoenix Corporation on their behalf?"

"And...?"

"And tried to convince them to renew my parents' loan."

"Ella—"

Once again Rafe cut Donald off. "Why would I do that?"

She glared at him. "Because they'll ruin my parents. They'd be stealing your idea. You have to stop them."

He stared at her in utter astonishment. Then he gave a short, rough laugh. "Ah, *amada*," he murmured. "You never cease to amaze me."

She lifted an eyebrow. "I gather that's not a compliment."

"No, I'm afraid not." He drummed his fingers on the tabletop. "Hasn't it occurred to you that I could be the one behind these financial difficulties?"

"No."

He looked intrigued. "Why not?"

"Because I trust you," she said simply. "You promised to give me time and you will."

"Ella—" her father began yet again.

"One moment, please," Rafe interrupted. All expression had dropped from his face and he stared at Ella with winter-gray eyes. "Then let me ask you this. Why would I step in? What difference does it make who takes your parents down when the end result is exactly what I'd hoped?"

She stalked across the room. Planting her hands on his desk, she leaned over the polished teak surface. "I'd think it would make a lot of difference. This Phoenix Corporation will have robbed you of your revenge. Besides, it's one thing for you to make the threat. We can discuss it like two rational adults and eventually I can get you to see reason. But this corporation—"

"Ella, you don't understand," Donald cut in.

She glanced over her shoulder. "What don't I understand?"

Rafe sighed. "I believe what your father is trying to say is that I own Phoenix Corporation. I'm the one causing your parents' financial woes. I did warn you I had the means, if you'll recall."

She straightened, stepping back from the desk. "No, I don't believe you."

Rafe glanced at Donald. "Would you excuse us for a moment? This won't take long. I'm sure Chelita is hovering nearby. Feel free to ask her for a cup of coffee."

The minute the door closed behind her father, Ella broke into speech. "Stop this, Rafe. I know you can."

"I can. But I won't."

She fought to keep her voice even. "If I gave you my word that there wouldn't be any further Cinderella Balls, would that be acceptable?"

"It isn't your word I need, but your parents'."

She stared at him as though she'd never seen him before. "Have you any idea why I came to Costa Rica? Any idea at all?"

He released a tired sigh. "We've been over this ground before. You're here to stop me from harming your parents. It's the same as I would have done if I'd been in your predicament. It's what I've been trying to do for Shayne ever since I took her away from Jackie."

"And this afternoon? Was making love to you another way of protecting my parents?"

His eyes narrowed. "If it was, it won't work."

"That you'd even think I could—" Every scrap of color drained from her face. "After all we've been through, you still don't trust me, do you?"

"I don't trust easily. You know that."

"But do you trust me?"

His control snapped and he surged to his feet. "Do you think I don't want to? I trusted you once before, remember? I let down my guard and trusted you with the one person who meant the most to me. And you betrayed me by inviting her to the Cinderella Ball. Is it any wonder that I hesitate to trust again? Is it any wonder that I'd do anything to stop these balls?"

"I guess not," she whispered.

He held out his hand. Where once his wedding band had glittered with a bright promise, now it appeared dark and somber. "Ella, our marriage doesn't have to end, if that's what concerns you. Once your father has given me the guarantee I've requested, we can be done with this matter. Our marriage can continue as before."

"Exactly how long will it continue? Forever?" He didn't answer, which was answer enough. "That's right. You don't believe in forever. Or miracles. Or love. Or happily-ever-after. Do you, Rafe?"

He closed his eyes. "No," he said bleakly. "I don't."

"I could make this so easy for you," she murmured. "But I refuse to do it."

"What are you talking about?"

She shook her head. "No, Rafe. I don't want half measures from you. It has to be all or nothing, which I guess leaves me with nothing. Now, if you'll excuse me, my father's waiting. I have to go."

"Go? What do you mean, go?"

She paused at the door. "I'm leaving, Rafe. I'm returning to Nevada. As far as your guarantee is concerned..." She looked over her shoulder with tarnished gold eyes. "You can go to hell."

A bitter smile touched his mouth. "It's too late, *amada*. I'm there already."

*   *   *

Shayne stepped from the shadows shading the courtyard fountain and approached Rafe. "You're staring at that mosaic of *La Estrella* like she holds the solution to all your problems," she commented.

"I wish that were so." He glanced down at what he held in his hand—Ella's unfolded wedding band. It was the only thing she'd left behind, a symbolic gesture that gleamed dully within his palm. "But it isn't."

Shayne watched him apprehensively. "You still don't trust her, do you?"

"Don't you start, too. Not now."

"Is it... Is it because of what happened at the Cinderella Ball?"

Rafe glanced at his sister, something in her voice capturing his full attention. He slipped the ring into his pocket. "Yes, the Cinderella Ball has a lot to do with it." He paused before asking with grave deliberation, "Or is it a mistake to hold that against her?"

Slowly Shayne nodded. "Yes," she whispered. "It is."

His gut tightened as the blinders were wrenched from his eyes. "She didn't invite you to the ball, did she? She didn't know you intended to find a husband."

"No," his sister confirmed, her voice almost inaudible.

But he heard. Heard and was forced to believe. "Ah, *mi pobrecita pichón*. Why have you kept this from me for so long?"

"Because..." Her chin quivered and she made a helpless gesture. "Because I was afraid."

"*Afraid*? Afraid of what?"

"Afraid that if I told you the truth, you'd hate me. That you'd get rid of me the way Jackie did."

"*Dios mío, nunca!*" He vaulted off the bench, sweeping her into his arms. "I'd never do such a thing. Surely you must realize this?"

She burrowed against him. "I'm sorry. It was wrong, I know. But I couldn't take the chance. You were all I had left."

"I swear, I will always be here for you." He caught her chin in his hand and forced her to look at him. "Nothing will ever change how I feel about you."

Tears filled her eyes. "I think I know that now."

"But you didn't then."

"No."

Jackie had a lot to pay for, far more than his wife ever would. "I can understand your remaining silent. But why didn't Ella tell me?"

"I asked her once. She said it was for your sake—that she didn't want to harm my relationship with you."

He swore beneath his breath, bitterly aware of how he'd misjudged his wife. If she were here now, they'd have a lengthy discussion on the subject. Unfortunately, he'd have to deal with that at a later date. For now he had other, more pressing concerns to address.

"Why did you do it?" he demanded. "Were you so unhappy with me? Was your life so terrible that you felt you had to marry in order to escape?"

"No, no. Just the opposite." Her tears spilled over. "My life was that wonderful. Don't you see? You came all the way to Florida looking for me. I wanted to find a man just like you, Rafe. Someone who would love me so much he'd go to the ends of the earth in search of me."

It was several minutes before he'd regained his control enough to speak. "You are mistaken," he told her hoarsely. "I am not such a man."

"Aren't you?" Shayne pulled free of his arms and fixed him with huge, dark eyes. "You think there's no such thing as happily-ever-after. But don't you get it? That's exactly what you gave me as a child."

"No. I failed you. Jackie—"

"Everything you've ever done has been out of love and the desire to protect me. Even Jackie."

"And McIntyre?"

"I found happily-ever-after with him, too. Briefly. Someday I'll find it again. And this time, I won't let anything take it from me."

Her admission ate at his soul like acid. "You still love him, don't you?"

She didn't spare his feelings. "With all my heart. Even if I never find love again, at least I had that one night." She gripped his hand. "I'll bet Ella feels the same way."

"Perhaps once," he said. "But no longer."

"You can't be certain of that. Don't lose this opportunity, Rafe. You'll regret it the rest of your life."

"I have no faith," he whispered, staring at the mosaic with empty eyes. "I don't believe. And she needs someone who does."

"Ella believes enough for the both of you." Her voice grew urgent. "Listen to me, Rafe. You have a decision to make. A very simple decision. Either you love and trust Ella enough to try and win her back. Or you don't. Now which is it?"

His hands folded into fists. "I don't think I can say the words she needs to hear."

"Then show her. Show her by making things right."

"You ask the impossible."

"Because of the Cinderella Balls? They're no longer an issue, now are they? Or is it that you suspect her motives for coming here? That's it, isn't it? You think she came for her parents' sake instead of for yours." She made an impatient sound. "Honestly, Rafe, I could slap you for being such a fool."

"What the hell are you talking about?"

"Do you really think Ella's feelings for her parents are any less than your feelings for me?"

He shook his head decisively. "No. They mean everything to her."

"And yet she put their future in danger by trying to gain your love instead of giving you an agreement to end the Cinderella Balls. Would you have been willing to risk as much if your positions had been reversed?"

It came to him then, with all the raw power of a lightning strike. Shayne was right. There could only be one reason Ella would put her parents in such financial jeopardy. And she'd been shouting it loud and clear from the moment he'd first walked back into her life. He just hadn't been listening.

His mouth twisted. "It would seem Donald Montague will have the last laugh, after all."

"About what?"

"He said it would be interesting to see which won out in our marriage—the head or the heart."

Shayne laughed in genuine amusement. "And you, of course, said the head."

Rafe gave a self-derisive smile. "Only because I was so certain I had no heart."

"Which just goes to prove..." She shot him an impish grin. "You aren't so perfect after all. I'm sure Ella will be vastly relieved to hear you admit it."

Ella stood in the middle of the glade behind her parents' house. She'd spent more time here in the week since she'd left Costa Rica than ever before.

She bowed her head and studied her ring finger. Where once there'd been a wedding band, now only a pale mark remained to underscore painful memories. It hurt to her very soul to discover she'd been wrong about Rafe and the Cinderella Ball. She'd wanted so much to believe in magic and miracles and fairy tales. But the time had come to face a bitter truth... She wasn't Cinderella any

more than she was *La Estrella*. To pretend otherwise only
led to heartbreak, as she'd so recently discovered.

"I thought I might find you here."

She lifted her head at the familiar-sounding voice,
afraid to look, afraid to discover her imagination had
played a nasty trick.

"Aren't you even going to say hello?" Rafe asked,
amusement rippling through his deep voice.

Steeling herself to face him, she turned. "Why have
you come? Or is that a foolish question?"

"A very foolish question, *amada*."

Her mouth tightened. "Don't call me that. Not
anymore."

"What would you rather I called you?" He raised an
eyebrow and approached. "*Dulzura? Mi alma? Mi
corazón?*"

"Stop it, Rafe. You don't mean any of those endear-
ments, so just stop."

"Or perhaps it would be more fitting to say...*La
Estrella*."

Her chin quivered. "I'm definitely not that."

"Have I stolen all your dreams, then?" he asked gently. "Have you no more faith?"

"Wasn't that the idea?" She drew a deep breath,
fighting for composure. "You must be here for your
agreement."

He shook his head. "I no longer need it."

"I see." That could only mean one thing. He knew
about the Cinderella Balls. Disappointment filled her.
She'd hoped he'd come because his love for her was so
overpowering it had surmounted all the obstacles that
stood between them—his anger, his mistrust, even his
hunger for revenge. But then, what had she expected?
A miracle? "In that case, I assume my father's already
spoken to you."

"Not yet, although we have quite a few matters to discuss, I would imagine."

"But you found out, didn't you? That's why you've returned?"

Slowly he shook his head. "You have lost me, *amada*. What is it I'm supposed to have discovered?"

"I'm talking about—" Her breath caught unexpectedly in a tiny, revealing break. "I'm talking about your finding out the truth."

His eyes narrowed. "And what truth is that?"

"That there aren't going to be any more Cinderella Balls. There never were!"

His brows snapped together. "Again, Ella. And more clearly this time."

A tiny flutter of some emotion, an emotion precariously close to hope fought for rebirth. "You're positive my father didn't say anything to you?"

"I've just told you that we haven't spoken," he replied impatiently. "Now what's going on? What has happened?"

"The night of the last Cinderella Ball, my mother revealed that she and Dad had decided to put an end to them. They'd gotten to an age where it was too difficult and stressful to organize such elaborate events." She gazed at him uncertainly. "You really didn't know?"

"*Madre de Dios*!" He reached her in two swift strides. "This is true?" he rasped, catching hold of her shoulders. "You knew from the beginning there would be no more balls?"

"Yes."

"Why did you not tell me? Why did you keep it a secret once I'd threatened—"

"Can't you guess?"

He closed his eyes and grimaced. "Hell. It's because you thought the truth would bring a rapid end to a hasty marriage, yes?"

"You'd have walked away and never looked back," she agreed.

"You're wrong. I was as consumed by you, as you were by me. If I'd walked, it wouldn't have been far, nor would I have been long returning." He gazed at her, his eyes like twin silver flames. "You were afraid, weren't you? Afraid that if you didn't marry, you'd lose your last opportunity for the Cinderella Ball to work its magic."

She glanced away. "I was a fool."

"Ella—"

"No! I don't want to hear it. You only came back because you wanted to see if your threat had worked."

He cupped the nape of her neck and forced her to look at him. "You will hear me, *amada*. I am not here for any such reason. No, don't argue with me. Just listen. As far as I was aware, you'd refused to give me my agreement and were willing to lose your home rather than cave to my demands."

It took every ounce of willpower not to lean forward and surrender to his warm strength. "You weren't wrong. We would have given in," she admitted. "In fact, Dad's been trying to reach you ever since we arrived home."

"To inform me there weren't going to be any more balls?"

"Yes." She closed her eyes. "I should have told you the truth before we left Costa Rica. For that matter, I should have told you right from the start. I—I was wrong to put my parents at risk."

"You were lucky it didn't go any further," he concurred. "And just so you know, I've paid off their loan."

"Saying thank you hardly seems adequate. But I do thank you." She eased from his arms and away from temptation. "We each have what we want now, don't we?"

"So there's no reason to continue our marriage, is that what you mean?" He wrapped an arm around her waist and pulled her back where she belonged. "Is it, *amada*?"

The tears fell then. "Please, Rafe," she whispered. "I can't bear any more. You have what you came for. Can't you just leave it at that and go?"

"No, I can't. You see, you took something that belonged to me when you left. It was something I didn't even realize I possessed until I'd lost it."

"I have nothing of yours," she instantly denied.

"You hold it tight within your grasp even as we speak."

She splayed her fingers. "I have nothing," she repeated.

He caught her wrists in an iron grip. "Please look again. For somewhere in these hands you've hidden my heart. And I would like to know that it's in safekeeping."

A sob tore at her throat. "Why have you come? Why have you really come?"

"It's difficult for me to say the words," he confessed in a low voice. "But I had hoped this might speak them for me."

Reaching into his pocket, he removed a small, square jeweler's box. She took it, shaking so badly she could barely manage to pry open the lid. Inside she found the wedding band she'd left behind. Only it had been repaired—and six colored gemstones encircled the ring, the largest a diamond.

He lifted the band from its velvet nest. "The smaller stones are for each of the Cinderella Balls that have been held since your birth."

She spoke through the tears blocking her throat. "And the diamond?"

"It is for the ball deserving the most recognition. The one where we wed. There's an inscription inside." She tilted the ring and in that instant hope dawned anew.

It read, "Happily-ever-after."

This time she couldn't stem the tears. She gestured toward his wedding band. "You've fixed yours, too."

He shrugged. "I am a rather crude jeweler. My ring kept snagging and I was afraid I would damage it."

"Does it also have an inscription?"

"It says..." He dragged air into his lungs, his eyes black with emotion. "It says, 'Forever.' For if such a thing exists, I would spend it with you."

She gazed up at him, her eyes as brilliant as the stars found in a midnight sky. "I promise you it does. And if you'll trust me just a little, I'll spend the rest of my life proving it to you."

"Ah, *amada*, my beloved wife." He lowered his mouth to capture hers. "I will trust you to keep that promise."

EPILOGUE

"RAFE, I'm fine," Ella insisted. "It's just a stitch. Nothing to worry about."

"Perhaps we should cancel the festivities." His accent deepened with worry. "You're in no condition—"

"We can't cancel the Anniversary Ball!" she protested. "It would disappoint so many people. They've been looking forward to this event for a full year. Besides, it's too late to cancel anything. Our guests are due to arrive any minute, whereas our baby isn't due for another two weeks."

He pulled her into his arms. "Naturally I would regret disappointing those who have come to celebrate their first anniversary with us. But my concern is for you and only you." He rested his hand on her swollen belly in a gesture as intimate and tender as it was familiar. From the day he'd learned of her pregnancy, he'd made a habit of holding her like this, his long fingers splayed across the gradually increasing expanse of her stomach.

"Our baby is active tonight," Rafe murmured. "Anxious to join the world."

"Anxious to meet his father, you mean."

"His? You assume a lot, *amada*. Perhaps we'll have a girl." A slow smile of satisfaction crept across his mouth. "To hold a daughter in my arms would make me a happy man."

She gazed at him anxiously. "Would a son also please you?"

"Very much, as you well know."

A light knock sounded at the door and Shayne peeked into the room. "Ella, your parents sent me. It's time. The first guests are just arriving."

"We'll be there in a moment," Rafe said. He waited until his sister left before adding, "She looks better, don't you think? Contented."

"She'll be fine, Rafe." Ella caressed the taut line of his jaw, feeling his tension ease beneath her loving touch. "Her mosaics are in constant demand. She just picked up three new commissions."

"Thanks to *La Estrella*," Rafe inserted. "You have been a busy woman performing all those miracles. Shayne has a career she adores. Milagro has become happy and prosperous—"

"That's just because you changed your mind about selling *Esperanza*. As for Shayne's personal life ... Give her time. That will come, too."

"With you working your magic, how can I doubt it?" He pulled Ella closer, resting his jaw against her temple. "I made a mistake six years ago," he confessed. "I took from her the one man she ever loved. That was wrong of me."

"You don't know that for certain," Ella replied gently. "None of us do. She was only seventeen. A mere child. You did what you thought necessary to protect her from harm."

"I should have given this McIntyre a chance. Perhaps it would have worked out between them."

"Regrets won't change the past." She kissed the worry from his expression. "Let it go, sweetheart."

"If you wish. For now." Rafe slipped a supportive hand around her waist and looked down at her, his eyes a brilliant shade of silver. "Come, *amada*. It's time to greet our guests. I have arranged for a chair to be placed at the head of the receiving line for you. You are to tell me if you experience so much as a twinge. Understood?"

She smiled, a smile full of love and joy. "Understood."

"Chick, if you'd let me get a word in edgewise I'll tell you how we first met," Jake Hondo groused.

"But is this where you got married? Is it?" the six-year-old demanded. "Right here?"

"They didn't get married on the sidewalk," Buster scoffed. "They did it inside. In that palace, over there." He waved a hand toward the cupcake castle in the distance.

"We did first meet on the sidewalk, though," Wynne inserted, ruffling Chick's pale blond hair.

"And I told her to get lost," Jake added dryly. "Not that she listened. Come to think of it, she still doesn't listen all that well."

Wynne chuckled. "You should be used to it by now."

"Damn—I mean, danged straight," he muttered soft enough that only she heard. "Though it's come as one heck of a shock to find my life ordered around by a pint-sized elf and three noisy kids."

She just grinned. "You can't fool me. You love every minute."

His gaze softened. "You've got that right. Every second of every minute of every hour of every day."

"You haven't finished the story," Chick complained, tugging on Jake's suit jacket.

"You've heard that story a thousand times," Wynne protested. "You don't really want to hear it again, do you?"

"He likes it. And so do I," Buster explained, before taking up the tale. "Then Uncle Jake married Aunt Wynne and found out about us. Boy howdy, he was ticked. You prob'ly don't remember 'cause you was too little."

"I do so remember! He cussed and Aunt Wynne yelled at him for cussin'."

Jake heaved an exaggerated sigh. "She still yells at me."

"There's a simple solution to that," Wynne retorted. "Stop cussin'."

"Spoilsport."

"I'm not done with the story!" Buster complained. "And then Uncle Jake saved you and me from freezin' to death. And got rid of mean Aunt Marsh. Then they had Tracy. And last of all named her after our Mom once she got borned. Isn't that how it happened?"

Jake grinned. "Something like that." As though in response to hearing her name, his three-month-old daughter gurgled in delight. He shifted her to his other arm and she fixed him with bright spring-green eyes beneath a mop of satiny black curls. He flicked her snub nose with a gentle finger. "Well, folks? We gonna stand out here jawing all day or do we go in and join the party? As I recall they have some mighty fine desserts in there."

"Desserts!" Chick and Buster shouted in unison.

A greedy light dawned in Wynne's eyes. "I'll second that. Lead the way."

"Jonah, there's something I want to tell you," Nikki began.

He wrapped an arm around her and pulled her close. "There's something I want to tell you, too. Care to guess?"

Her gaze slid downward, examining the line of his trousers. "You didn't—"

A suggestive grin spread across his mouth. "No, as a matter of fact, I didn't. But that's not what I wanted to tell you." They reached the entrance to the ballroom and he brushed her mouth with a quick kiss. "Afraid it'll have to keep."

"But, I—"

"Hang on, love." Jonah offered his hand to Rafe Beaumont, then introduced Nikki. "So, we meet again."

"Under more congenial circumstances, I hope," Rafe replied.

Jonah glanced at a very pregnant Ella and his grin widened. "Most definitely. I'm relieved to see the two of you worked out your problems."

Amusement crept into Rafe's voice. "Or added to them."

"With children, you never know," Jonah acknowledged. "Scares the hell out of me."

"You aren't alone, my friend," Rafe said wryly. "Enjoy your visit."

Jonah caught Nikki's hand in his and guided her into the crowded ballroom. "Come on, honey. Let's dance." His hazel eyes gleamed suggestively. "Remember the last time we danced here?"

"Is that what you call it? I thought it was a blatant attempt to seduce me."

He gave his most innocent look as he swung her onto the floor. "Isn't that the point?"

"It certainly was a year ago." She sighed as their bodies melded, moving together in perfect harmony. "Jonah... We never did finish our conversation."

"Too true, my love. What were we discussing? Ah, I remember. Undergarments."

"No, you were discussing undergarments. I was discussing—"

"Well, hello there," a cheery voice interrupted from the edge of the dance floor. "Remember me?"

Nikki turned, searching her memory for a name. "Of course I remember. Wynne, isn't it? Wynne Sommers?"

"It's Hondo, now."

"I was nervous about finding a husband and you let me practice on—" Her gaze switched to Jake and she gave a chagrined laugh. "Oops. Hi, again."

"She let you practice on me, did she?" Jake asked dryly. "Now why doesn't that surprise me?"

"It was harmless," Wynne insisted blithely, cradling their baby against her shoulder. "You weren't ready to admit defeat and marry me. And Nikki needed to get over her nervousness. Hey, have you tried the desserts yet? They're—"

"Hang on, elf," Jake interrupted. "I think there's a lady behind you who needs some help."

Nikki glanced over her husband's shoulder, her breath catching in a soft gasp. "Oh, Jonah. It's Ella Beaumont."

"Looks like she's gone into labor," Wynne predicted. "Let's go see what we can do."

The four hurried to Ella's side. She stood in the doorway between the ballroom and the salons, clinging to the wooden frame as though her life depended on it.

"Easy, Mrs. Beaumont." Jake gently lifted her into his arms. "Looks like you could use a ride to the hospital."

"My husband," she gasped. "I need Rafe."

"You need to get to the hospital," Wynne corrected gently.

"I'll find your husband and let him know what's happened," Jonah offered. "We'll be in the next car out of here. I promise."

"You do enjoy playing the knight in shining armor," Ella murmured with a pained smile.

"I'm not sure it's a role I enjoy. Just one I seem to get stuck with." Jonah glanced at Jake. "Can you get her to the hospital?"

"No problem. Wynne, drag the boys away from that dessert table and we're out of here."

"Do you mind if we stick around a while longer?" Nikki asked a short time later. She took a seat in the waiting room "I don't want to leave the hospital until I'm sure Ella and the baby are both okay."

"Mrs. Beaumont seemed to be handling it like a trooper." Jonah ruffled her auburn curls and chuckled. "If you want to worry about anyone, save your concern for Mr. Beaumont."

"Did you understand anything he said?"

"Aside from *rapido*? Not a word. My Spanish is a bit rusty—which I believe is just as well." He shook his head. "This is not an ordeal I'm anxious to experience."

Nikki gripped her hands together. "Listen, Jonah—"

"Hi, again," Wynne greeted them, excitement sparkling in her bright green eyes. "Did you decide to hang around, too? Do you mind some company?"

"Not at all," Jonah replied. "The more the merrier."

"Jonah—"

"With all these kids, I can supply the more," Wynne said with a chuckle. "If you'll supply the merry. I wonder if Ella will take as long to deliver as I did. I swear, I was in that labor room for a solid week."

Jake leaned against the door jamb between the waiting area and the hallway. "Doesn't look like we'll have quite that long to wait. Beaumont's on his way right now."

"Jonah," Nikki tried again, exasperation edging her voice.

Rafe walked in and grinned. "I just wanted to stop by and tell you Ella had a boy. I'd offer cigars, but I fear my wife would not approve. So instead I offer you my most sincere thanks and appreciation."

"Jonah—"

"Congratulations, Beaumont." Jonah stuck out his hand. "We were happy to help."

"Honey—"

"I guess we'll be leaving now," Wynne said. "It's time we got our troop to bed. Please give Ella our best."

"Jonah!"

Rafe inclined his head. "Of course. If you'll excuse me. I have a wife and son waiting me."

"Jonah!" Nikki shouted. "I'm pregnant, dammit."

"Hey, lady. You're not supposed to cuss," Chick informed her earnestly.

"I know and I'm sorry." She looked at Jonah apprehensively. "I've...I've been trying to tell you all evening. But we keep getting interrupted."

"In that case, we'll be going," Wynne said firmly. She gave Nikki a quick hug and kiss. "Take care of yourself. And stay in touch."

And then they were alone.

"You're pregnant?" Jonah demanded. "With a baby?"

"That's the normal procedure," Nikki said tearfully. "Unless you know something I don't."

"Why...why didn't you tell me? I mean, before tonight. You must have known."

"I've been trying to work up the nerve. I—I didn't think you wanted a baby."

"Didn't want...?" He closed his eyes. When he looked at her again it was with such fierce desire that her tears overflowed. He hauled her into his arms. "I'm sorry. I'm sorry I ever gave you that impression since it's the furthest thing from the truth. I love you, Nikki. And the thought of you carrying my child..." He touched her with gentle tenderness, his enthralled expression giving weight to his words. "This is the best gift you've ever given me."

"Even better than tickets to the Anniversary Ball?" she teased.

"Those come close." His hand sank into her hair and he feathered a kiss across her mouth. "But only because this is where it all began for us. And where—it would seem—it continues."

* * *

"Isn't he beautiful?" Ella whispered, stroking her son's cheek with a gentle finger.

Rafe peered over her shoulder. "If you like things that are small, red and squished, he's attractive enough I suppose."

"Rafe!"

"I am joking. He's the most beautiful son I've ever had. Of course, he's also the only son I've ever had." He hesitated, tucking a stray lock of hair behind her ear. "There is something I have been meaning to tell you for a very long time."

Busily counting fingers and toes, Ella simply nodded.

"I love you, *amada*. I love you with all my heart and soul."

She stilled, instantly losing count. "What did you say?"

"I said, I love you." He frowned pensively. "I do not know why I found the words so difficult to say when actually, they come with ease— *Amada*, why are you crying? Is there something wrong? Should I call a nurse?"

She shook her head, wiping her cheeks before she soaked the baby. "No, you just caught me by surprise. I love you, too, Rafe."

He stole a slow, gentle kiss. "I am finding that it is as good to hear the words as it is to say them."

"I'm glad you finally came to that conclusion. You have a lot of catching up to do, you know."

"I'll go to work on it right away, I promise."

"We should call my parents and Shayne and let them know about the baby." She caught his frown and understood the cause. "Don't worry. Her chance will come again. The happiness we've found, she'll find, too."

"It is possible..." He took a deep breath and then said, "It is possible she will find love at the next Cinderella Ball."

It took a full minute for his words to sink in. "What did you say?"

"The next Cinderella Ball. Maybe Shayne will—"

Tears welled up in her eyes again, turning them to molten gold. "Do you mean it? You're willing to carry on my parents' tradition?"

"How could I not? The money goes to a good cause. And from the research I've done these past months, there has only been one marriage to fail in all the years your parents have held the ball."

"Shayne's?"

"Technically, it cannot be considered a failure, since the marriage was not legal."

"Rafe?"

He sighed. "I am...I am willing to give it a try, *amada*, if you are. And perhaps..."

"Perhaps?"

"Perhaps we don't have to wait a full five years."

Harlequin Romance ®

brings you

Authors you'll treasure, books you'll want to keep!

Harlequin Romance books just keep getting better and better...and we're delighted to welcome you to our Simply the Best showcase for 1997.

Each month for a whole year we'll be highlighting a particular author—one we know you're going to love!

Watch for:

#3445 *MARRY ME*
by Heather Allison

TV presenter Alicia Hartson is a romantic: she believes in Cupid, champagne and roses, and Mr. Right. Tony Domenico is not Mr. Right! He's cynical, demanding and unromantic. Where Alicia sees happy endings, her boss sees ratings. But they do say that opposites attract, and it is Valentine's Day!

Available in February wherever
Harlequin books are sold.

1997
Reader's Engagement Book
A calendar of important dates
and anniversaries for readers to use!

Informative and entertaining—with notable
dates and trivia highlighted throughout the year.

Handy, convenient, pocketbook size to help you
keep track of your own personal important dates.

Added bonus—contains $5.00 worth of coupons
for upcoming Harlequin and Silhouette books.
This calendar more than pays for itself!

 Available beginning in November at
your favorite retail outlet.

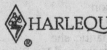

Harlequin Romance ®

brings you

BABY BOOM

We are proud to announce the birth of our new bouncing baby series—Baby Boom!

Each month in 1997 we'll be bringing you your very own bundle of joy—a cute, delightful romance by one of your favorite authors. Our heroes and heroines are about to discover that two's company and three (or four...or five) is a family!

This exciting new series is all about the true labor of love...

Parenthood, and how to survive it!

Watch for:
#3443 *THREE LITTLE MIRACLES*
by Rebecca Winters

Tracey couldn't forget the devastating secret that had forced her to run out on Julien Chappelle four days after their honeymoon. What she hadn't counted on was that her brief marriage had left more than memories. A set of adorable triplets who needed their mom to come home! It seemed Tracey had only one motive for leaving, and three reasons to stay....

Available in February wherever Harlequin books are sold.

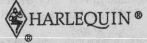

HARLEQUIN®

Don't miss these Harlequin favorites by some of our most distinguished authors!
And now, you can receive a discount by ordering two or more titles!

HT#25645	THREE GROOMS AND A WIFE by JoAnn Ross	$3.25 U.S. $3.75 CAN.	☐ ☐
HT#25647	NOT THIS GUY by Glenda Sanders	$3.25 U.S. $3.75 CAN.	☐ ☐
HP#11725	THE WRONG KIND OF WIFE by Roberta Leigh	$3.25 U.S. $3.75 CAN.	☐ ☐
HP#11755	TIGER EYES by Robyn Donald	$3.25 U.S. $3.75 CAN.	☐ ☐
HR#03416	A WIFE IN WAITING by Jessica Steele	$3.25 U.S. $3.75 CAN.	☐ ☐
HR#03419	KIT AND THE COWBOY by Rebecca Winters	$3.25 U.S. $3.75 CAN.	☐ ☐
HS#70622	KIM & THE COWBOY by Margot Dalton	$3.50 U.S. $3.99 CAN.	☐ ☐
HS#70642	MONDAY'S CHILD by Janice Kaiser	$3.75 U.S. $4.25 CAN.	☐ ☐
HI#22342	BABY VS. THE BAR by M.J. Rodgers	$3.50 U.S. $3.99 CAN.	☐ ☐
HI#22382	SEE ME IN YOUR DREAMS by Patricia Rosemoor	$3.75 U.S. $4.25 CAN.	☐ ☐
HAR#16538	KISSED BY THE SEA by Rebecca Flanders	$3.50 U.S. $3.99 CAN.	☐ ☐
HAR#16603	MOMMY ON BOARD by Muriel Jensen	$3.50 U.S. $3.99 CAN.	☐ ☐
HH#28885	DESERT ROGUE by Erine Yorke	$4.50 U.S. $4.99 CAN.	☐ ☐
HH#28911	THE NORMAN'S HEART by Margaret Moore	$4.50 U.S. $4.99 CAN.	☐ ☐

(limited quantities available on certain titles)

	AMOUNT	$
DEDUCT:	**10% DISCOUNT FOR 2+ BOOKS**	$
ADD:	**POSTAGE & HANDLING**	$
	($1.00 for one book, 50¢ for each additional)	
	APPLICABLE TAXES*	$_____
	TOTAL PAYABLE	$_____
	(check or money order—please do not send cash)	

To order, complete this form and send it, along with a check or money order for the total above, payable to Harlequin Books, to: **In the U.S.:** 3010 Walden Avenue, P.O. Box 9047, Buffalo, NY 14269-9047; **In Canada:** P.O. Box 613, Fort Erie, Ontario, L2A 5X3.

Name: _____

Address: _____ City: _____

State/Prov.: _____ Zip/Postal Code: _____

*New York residents remit applicable sales taxes.
 Canadian residents remit applicable GST and provincial taxes.
Look us up on-line at: http://www.romance.net

HBACK-JM4